Saving Logan

Scarred Hero Romance

Kaci Rose

Five Little Roses Publishing

Copyright

Copyright © 2023, by Kaci Rose, Five Little Roses Publishing. All Rights Reserved.

No part of this publication may be reproduced, distributed,
or transmitted in any form or by any means, including photocopying, recording,
or other electronic or mechanical methods, or by any information storage and
retrieval system without the prior written permission of the publisher, except
in the case of very brief quotations embodied in critical reviews and certain
other noncommercial uses permitted by copyright law.

Publisher's Note: This is a work of fiction. Names, characters, places, and incidents are a product of the author's imagination.
Locales and public names are sometimes used for atmospheric purposes. Any
resemblance to actual people, living or dead, or to businesses, companies,

.tions, or locales is completely coinciden-

Editing By: Debbe @ **On The Page, Author and PA Services**

Proofread By: Laura Bowles

Dedication

To all the men and women serving our country, past and present. To their friends and families who support them daily.

Contents

Get Free Books!

Do you like Military Men? Best friends brothers?
What about sweet, sexy, and addicting books?

If you join Kaci Rose's Newsletter you get these books free!

https://www.kacirose.com/free-books/
Now on to the story!

Chapter 1

Logan

I know my voice is gone. I do.

But to unlearn a habit you've been doing your whole life by simply opening your mouth to speak is a little harder to undo. Every time my doctor or nurses asks me a question, I open my mouth and try to speak.

Then I get the looks of pity. Pity that I can't speak anymore. Pity that I can't remember that I can't speak anymore. Pity for the poor disabled man that they have to deal with day in and day out. Though I'm sure some of that pity is for themselves because when I realize I can't speak anymore, I just get angry all over again.

I guess that's why the hospital shipped me here to Oakside. They described it as the in-between place. While I don’t really need the hospital anymore, I still need help to get back on my feet.

Yesterday, I checked in and got my room. It was a relief to see it. Actually, it feels more like a bed-and-breakfast than a hospital. Not only do I have my own room, but there are hardwood floors, and my own private bathroom. Since there's nothing wrong with my legs other than I have to regain my strength, I was put on the second floor, so the views aren't even half bad.

The bathroom has black and white tile on the floor, and the walls are a light gray with white accents, making it nice and bright in the bathroom. I have a desk that I can sit and work while I look out of the window. There's also a comfortable little seating area with a TV, a couch, and a couple of chairs on the opposite side of the area where my bed and dresser are. Also, I have a small counter with a coffeepot and room for some snacks as well. All in all, the room is much better than everything that I thought I would find. If I had to pick between here and the hospital, I would definitely choose to stay here.

The other benefit is that all my doctor's appointments are here, along with my physical therapy appointments and any other therapists I might need. They plan to bring in someone to help me learn how to communicate with the outside world now that I can't speak, and they have someone to help me transition into the civilian world since the military doesn't want me anymore.

The military is all I've ever known, so I have no idea how they plan to do get that accomplished. But apparently, they've worked miracles in the past.

I'm pulled out of my thoughts by a knock on the door. Turning, I look to see who it was.

"Is it okay if I come in?" Lexi asks.

When I nod, she smiles and comes to sit on the couch on the opposite side of the room from me. She's always given me plenty of space.

"I wanted to come and see how you were doing. The teacher we brought in to teach you ASL and how to communicate with the outside world is here, and I wanted to make sure you were up for meeting with her. While you can't put it off forever, if you aren't up for it this week, we could push it off to next week to give you more time to get settled."

One of the things I like about Oakside is that Lexi and her husband are the owners. It's an old plantation home that has been turned into a rehabilitation center for injured military members. When I got here, the nurse told me that Lexi used to live here on her own before she got the idea to turn it into what it is now. To give up such a beautiful home for all of us, I know she has to be a kind person.

Forgetting for just a moment that I can't speak, I went to again open my mouth to say yes. Instead, I just nod my head. At least Lexi is one of the few people around here that does not give me a look of pity. I really appreciate that more than she will ever know.

"Okay, so her name is Faith. I'll go get her and bring her up here. I think you two will really get along." She smiles, jumping up from where she's sitting, and leaves.

Taking a deep breath, I make my way over to the couch to sit. I know this woman is trying to help, supposedly like all the doctors and nurses before her. But when you can't talk and you are so lost in your own head, is there really anyone that can pull you out of it?

Lexi had brought Faith in to meet me earlier last week. It was a short meeting, but all I remember is that she was the most beautiful woman I have ever seen. She looked like Mandy Moore and was just as stunning. Even though I'm sure Lexi remembers the meeting, I think she was reminding me of her name in case I forgot. Ironically, I don't have anyone to tell or any way to even say that there's no way I'd forget a single detail about the gorgeous Faith.

As I think about working with her this week, my nerves start to really rack up. Before the accident, I would not have hesitated to ask her out, and I'd have loved flirting with her. But now, I have no game because I have no voice.

When she steps into the room, she pauses in the doorway and smiles. Our eyes lock for just a minute and I know it's completely in my head, but it feels like we have had a 'moment.'

Trying to shake it off, I focus on her.

"May I come in?" she asks. I still remember to this day her beautiful voice, even though I've only heard her speak a few times well over a week ago.

I nod my head, and if it's even possible, her smile grows. She takes a seat in the chair next to where I'm sitting. The couch and both of the chairs in the sitting area are leather, and I have to admit they are quite comfortable. But after watching her sit down and sink into the chair, it gives me dirty thoughts of other things and ways we could use the chair.

Mentally, I shake my head, trying to focus on the curvy bombshell in front of me. She places a folder on her lap and opens it to look it over. My guess is it's my medical folder that has followed me from the hospital here. Every doctor or nurse and pretty much anyone that interacts with me here at Oakside has looked at it.

"So today is kind of a get-to-know-you session and figure out your needs so I can make a plan for us going forward. I just want to verify some information in here. While I know you've probably done this a bunch of times since you've been here, but please bear with me, okay?" she asked, giving me an apologetic smile.

When I nod, she continues.

"So it says that you were injured in a plane crash and that you were in and out of it for roughly four months after?" she asks, looking at me.

Again, I just nod.

"Do you remember any of the time in that four months waking up or anything?"

Shaking my head no, because I don't remember it. What I do remember is the panic of the plane going down and then waking up in a stateside hospital. At some point, even though I was unconscious, I guess I was stable enough to be moved from Germany here, but I don't remember a single part of it.

"There's a note in here that the pilot who was with you also survived. He's here at Oakside as well, having lost his sight. Have the two of you seen... ah... interacted with each other?" She catches herself and a little blush crosses her cheeks.

I can only imagine how weird it is to have to adjust your normal ways of saying things around the men here.

Again, I nod my head. I go in and see Jenkins every few days. Sometimes his wife, Melody, is there, and she will do a bit of translating for us. He'll speak and I'll either nod my head or write on my whiteboard and his wife will read it off.

If his wife wasn't there, then Lexi would have been amazing at coming in and translating for us.

"Have to be honest, I've never worked with someone who has lost their voice the way you have. So, this is a bit of a learning process for us both. So, you will have to bear with me."

Once again I nod, not sure what else I can say. It's not like I have a choice and of course, I want her to keep coming back. If nothing else, she is easy to look at and might be able to understand what I'm going through.

She sets the folder on the coffee table before turning to look at me.

"Do you know any sign language?" she asks. But this time as she speaks, she used her hands.

I'm watching her hands instead of really concentrating on the question.

"As I talk, my hands will use sign language. You'll get used to it and will start seeing some repetitive signs. It's kind of like when you move to a new country and you immerse yourself in the language."

I heard many of the guys I served with say the same thing when they were stationed overseas, so I just nod my head.

"Do you know any sign language?" she asks. Again, I shake my head no.

"I know it sucks writing everything down, but as we go, you'll learn more and it'll get a lot easier to communicate," she says.

Then, reaching into the bag next to the chair, she pulls out a spiral-bound brown notebook and a pen and hands them to me. Carefully, I take it from her. Reaching into her bag again, she pulls out one that looks exactly like it, except this one is a dark blue.

"I want you to write down anything and everything. Whatever is on your mind that you want to get out, including any questions or concerns that you have. Think about the things you normally talk to people about, but can't right now. Anything that you want me to know, put it in there. I'll write in mine, and we'll swap them at every visit. Write as much or as little as you want."

I run my hands over the soft leather of the cover. Even when I was deployed, I never really wrote letters. Mostly I'd stuck to emails, not that I had a lot of people to email.

"The more we talk, the more you will pick up different signs, and the easier sign language will become. But you have to remember there are always going to be people in your life that don't know sign language. There are constantly going to be barriers to communication, but my job is to teach you how to overcome them."

I've had many nights to think about how this is my life now. There will be constant barriers to communication. Either I write long sentences on a whiteboard or in a notebook to hand to people and watch as they get impatient, or I don't communicate at all.

Even though I don't know how she thinks she's going to make it any easier, but if it means her coming around more often, I'll try this.

Chapter 2

Faith

There's just something in Logan's eyes that draws me to him. Every day since we had our initial meeting last week, I've seen those eyes. I can't escape them no matter how hard I try. Those captivating honey-colored eyes I see every time I close my eyes.

His dark reddish brown hair has grown out longer than a military cut. Since he's been injured, he's got a nice looking beard. Pair it with the tattoos that I can see on his arms, and what girl wouldn't swoon? But I can't let that affect me and the treatment that I give him.

I have to stay professional. Even if under any other circumstances, I'd be trying to flirt with them. Well, that's a lie. I'd probably be a little too shy to flirt with him, but if he showed any interest, then I would.

He doesn't realize it, but his eyes and his face just say so much more if you know how to read him. That's what I learned to do in school, read people to anticipate their needs.

"You feel isolated, Don't you?" I ask him, signing with my hands.

Once again, he nods, but this time he looks down at his feet.

It's not easy for people to open up, especially to be vulnerable after an accident like his. If they are not able to open up and allow themselves to be vulnerable before the accident, it's even harder after. What all this means is I have a completely uphill battle with him. One that I look forward to fighting.

Finally, I pull out another simple black leather journal from my bag.

"This one is for you to write whatever you want. No one will read this one. Use it to get your frustrations out when you get angry at a situation or just need to express yourself somehow. Many of my clients have found that they write in it, and then burn it, making them feel so much better."

He picks up the whiteboard that's sitting next to him and writes on it before turning it around to face me.

Thank you.

Taking a moment, I show him the sign for thank you and he masters it really fast.

"You're welcome."

He erases the dry-erase board and sets it on his lap. He seems open to talking, so now might be my time to get more information from him.

"Is there anyone at home that also needs to learn sign language and different ways to be able to communicate with you?" I ask. He just shakes his head.

"Any family or siblings?" I ask and again it's a no.

"Girlfriend or wife?" I ask. All the while knowing I don't need to because I'm sure he would have said if there was. But part of me wants to know if there's someone else in his life, even if it's completely unprofessional curiosity.

Again, he shakes his head and the amount of relief I feel lets me know that this is not professional. I need to rein it in, but I still have more to go over with him today.

He picks up the whiteboard and starts writing again. This time, it takes him a bit longer. He glances up at me a few times, but I just offer him a smile. I could be as patient as he needs and I know when you have a lot to say and you have to write it out, some people aren't very patient. When he finally turns the board around, it takes me a minute to read it.

It was just me and my grandparents growing up. But they have since passed away. I have no other family. Only friends I have were in the military.

I nod, but he holds up his finger, and he erases the whiteboard and starts writing again. It's filled a second time and then he flips it around.

My best friend was on the plane with me. He's here at Oakside and has lost his sight. Sign language won't help us.

I've never felt my heart crack so completely.

"I promise you we will find a way for you to communicate. My friend Lauren is here and I believe she's the one working with him. I'll talk with her. Her fiancé also lost his sight serving in the military. She helped him and he's going to be helping your friend as well. There are plenty of people here who understand what you're going through even if they have never been in your exact situation."

I know that he's probably heard that many times before since he's been here, but it is the truth. I hope he experiences that soon. If nothing else, for sure he would see it with Lexi and Noah. Noah was in the military himself and had massive burns on one side of his body. His face and his arms are the most visible. Now he wears them like a badge of honor. Though I know it took him a long time to get there.

When he looks away, I don't know what else to say.

"I'm really sorry you're going through all this and don't have someone by your side to help you. But now you have me." I probably could have worded that better and kept my words more professional.

But when he looks back at me, the tears in his eyes are visible, and I know he needed it. Seeing such a strong man on the verge of crying is almost too much to handle.

Without a second thought, I go against everything that I have been trained to do and not do, getting up to sit beside him on the couch and pull him in for a hug.

At first, he tries to fight me. It's as if he shouldn't need the support or shouldn't need me, but I just hold him tighter and after a few more seconds he melts into me and holds me back just as tight. His entire body heaves as he sobs silently.

His face is buried in my neck, and I can feel the tears against my skin, which for whatever reason, triggers my own. But I will not let on to him that I'm crying because he needs my support and strength more than anything right now. Holding him tightly, I silently let him know I'm here for him.

At the same time, I tried to think of anything at all to push the tears in my own eyes away. Only that leads me down the dangerous path of thinking how such a rough and tumble man is crying in my arms. His tattooed arms are wrapped around me holding me tight, and I realize just how much I have thrown myself into work and neglected any type of relationship.

I had thought I was perfect for this job because I had absolutely no feelings for the men that I was working with. Hell, that's why it was easy to be a twenty-four-year-old and never had a very long relationship. I have never felt what I'm feeling now, and it's very disorienting especially, when my main focus should be my job and the client in front of me.

Then again, I've never had a man like Logan wrapping his arms around me. I've never felt so tiny in someone's arms. For one thing, my curves have always been a problem. After my prom date said that I'm fucking the fat girl and would be doing me a favor, I pretty much stopped dating. Not that anyone has really shown any interest in me since.

In order to change my thoughts, I think about a few of the clinical rotations I did and some of the nasty injuries

I've seen. The gorier the better, and that seems to calm my libido quite a bit.

At least enough that by the time Logan pulls back, I've have myself well composed. Offering him a shy smile, he shakes his head, picks up the whiteboard and starts writing.

I'm so sorry. I don't know what came over me.

"The healing process is a journey. You're going to have good days, bad days and you're going to have moments where you just need a shoulder. That's why I'm here. And don't forget about all the other people of Oakside who are here for you. Don't you ever feel like you have to apologize for needing a moment of comfort from someone? At least, not here," I tell him and again he nods.

Thank you, he signs.

"*You are welcome*," I sign back, smiling brilliantly.

"Before I go today, I have one more thing for you." I get up and go to my chair, needing to put some space between us. Then I reach into my bag and pull out a tablet.

"This is on loan from Oakside, but you are free to use it while you are here. I have a bunch of sign language videos, some of the basics already saved on here for you. So you could start watching them and learning tonight. There's also a program on here that will allow you to type and it will speak for you. It might be a bit faster than writing everything out. Plus, you can write things ahead of time like if you have something you want to say to the nurse or Lexi or myself and it will be there and ready when you need it."

I take the time to show him how to use all of it before gathering my stuff and leaving. On the way out, I get stopped by Lexi. Lauren told me to expect this, as she's always wanting updates to know how people are doing and how she can help.

"How's Logan?" she asks. There's genuine concern in her eyes. I can only imagine how hard it is to run a center like this while legitimately caring for each person who comes through. It has to be emotionally taxing. But that's also what makes her the perfect person to be in charge of a place like this, because she really truly cares.

"He had his first breakdown. Considering we just started today, it was not unexpected. Though I'm not quite sure what triggered it. I sat there for a few minutes with him and he sobbed. I gave him a few tools to start working with and the same videos that I gave you guys to start learning. At this point, how fast he goes is completely up to him and how dedicated he is to studying. If Noah could go in there and maybe study with him, it might make it more fun. It might be a great incentive for Logan."

"I'll make sure it happens. If you need anything from me for him, you make sure to let me know. We want to make sure that we have anything that could help. Also, don't forget that we have a budget set aside for things that he might need in his recovery. As you are aware, he's the first patient needing help with speech, so we want to accommodate him. Just let us know."

I know she's just trying to be helpful, but if that alone doesn't put pressure on me, I have no idea what would.

Chapter 3

Logan

As she walks out of the room, I can feel the loss of her presence almost immediately. The overwhelming sense of being alone hits me hard this time. Much harder than ever before.

Taking a few moments, I fiddle with the tablet she got me and the program that will speak for me. Once I'm pretty sure I have it figured out, I take it and go downstairs to Jenkins's room.

As I get there, his wife is just leaving. She smiles at me, leaning in to give me a hug.

"Ken is doing pretty well today, but I think he will definitely benefit from your visit."

Ken Jenkins and I were in boot camp together. When we got accepted to pilot school together, it was a miracle beyond miracles we got stationed together. We got even luckier when the leaders saw how well we worked together and they paired us to fly together. It turned out to be a blessing first and now a curse that will haunt us both.

"Baby, Logan is here," she calls over her shoulder into the room.

"Shoot. Aren't you leaving to pick the kids up from school? Do you think you can get a nurse before you go to translate for us?" Ken asks.

But I get Melody's attention and shake my head before starting to type on the tablet.

"Not necessary. I have a new toy to play with," the robotic AI voice speaks from the tablet. Hearing it, Ken laughs.

"Well, come sit down and let me get used to your new voice."

Melody gives me another hug before I go sit down on the opposite side of the couch from where Ken is. So that he can hear where I'm at and have an idea of what's going on, I always make sure to make extra noise.

"So I guess you met with that girl again, huh?" he says, referring to Faith.

"Yes, I even have homework. Journaling and watching videos," the tablet says for me.

"Man, I got homework too. I'm supposed to memorize the layout of my room. While I know the basics, I'm expected to know every detail. Melody was helping me, but she had to go pick the kids up."

"I don't think I'll be much help, but I'm happy to do what I can," I tell him via the tablet.

"Nah man, I'm just happy to sit here and chat. So, this girl Faith, you think she's going to be able to help you?"

"I hope so. She's off to a pretty good start and seems to be able to pull emotion out of me even when I want to hide." Once again, the tablet speaks for me.

"What do you mean?" he asks, his face getting serious.

"Well, she asked if anyone in my life needed to learn sign language. Any family, friends, wife or girlfriend. I said no, because the only person I had was you. So sign language would be useless between us. Then my brain went to who would want to be with me anyway and I just emotionally broke down and cried for the first time."

"Ah, that sucks man, but with your fancy new voice here I think we're going to do okay. And you will find someone. This place is full of success stories. You'll be finding someone or leaving here. Your life will go on."

"Not being able to see someone is one thing. Hell, girls probably like they don't have to worry about looking perfect all the time. A missing limb? No big deal. But not being able to communicate with someone, that's a whole different level." I type it out and thankfully, Jenkins is patient with me. He's one of the few people that have been.

"It's only a communication issue if you let it be. Oh, look at us. We're communicating just fine right now. You're going to learn sign language and you'll be able to communicate even better with the people around you. The right woman will either know sign language when you meet her or be willing to learn for you. If she isn't willing to work with the language barrier, then she's not the one, man. You'll find a way to make it work."

While I know he's right, I guess I don't have hope that the one is out there for me. Yet as I say that, visions of Faith pop into my head. Her gentle smile, her wavy brown hair and her beautiful amber eyes come to mind.

It's nice to be able to communicate with Jenkins, even if it is slow. He tells me all about what's going on in his life and with his kids at school. They're both in preschool, but man, they have busier schedules than we did in the military.

Come dinnertime, he lets me lead him to into the dining room and thankfully Lexi comes over and explains what food they have. We grab what we want and then find a table. After we eat, I walk him back to his room and then head back upstairs to mine.

Once alone yet again, I sit at the desk with both of the journals that Faith gave me earlier. Even though I should probably choose to write in the one that she won't read, there's something about being able to express my feelings and have someone actually know how I feel that really appeals to me right now.

Picking up the journal that she said we would exchange and the pen that she left with it, I open the soft leather cover to the front page. A nice bright white lined piece of paper greets me. I just stare at it. Though I'm not quite sure where to start, I know that I need to write, and begin.

I know she's going to be expecting it as part of my healing. But I have an almost unbearable need to communicate with someone after being trapped inside my head for so long.

Placing the date at the top of the paper, I hesitate, unsure of what to write. Once again, I'm looking at the page in front of me. After staring at it for what seems like hours, I'm taken out of my trance by a knock on the door. Looking up, I see Lexi standing there.

"I just wanted to check on you before I head home. Faith gave us the same sign language videos that she gave you so that we could learn as well. We assigned you both a daytime and nighttime nurse that are both fluent in sign language. Don't be afraid to use it as you learn and they're happy to help too. Just so you know, your doctor, physical therapist, and therapists are all fluent in sign language. We have scheduled extra time for your appointments as you learn so that you have time to type out on the tablet or write out anything that you need. Your appointments start tomorrow and your nurse will let you know your schedule in the morning. Now that you are all settled, do you need or want anything before I leave?"

Taking a moment to digest what she's said, I can't think of anything. If I needed to know something, a nurse wouldn't be able to help me, so I shake my head and smile at her. After returning the smile, she leaves.

When she's gone, I turn back to the piece of paper in front of me.

Faith,

Not being able to communicate with those around me leaves me stuck in my head. Right now, that is a very scary place to be. I've never been much of a writer, but the pages of this journal call to me.

Maybe it's because I know that this is my life now. Will I be constantly writing things down for people around me? Or maybe I am just desperate to get my thoughts out of my head and for someone to know them.

My time to get settled here at Oakside is over and now I have to start seeing my doctors and a therapist. This means I will have to talk about what it was like to go down in that plane crash. Honestly, I don't know all of it. I remember the instruments malfunctioning and the plane starting to go down. Though I do remember the sheer panic that I felt and Jenkins yelling on the radio, trying to get anybody's attention, hoping someone would hear and save us.

But the crash itself, I don't remember. Nor do I recall the times they say I woke up during the four months before I was really conscious. By the time I woke up, I was already stateside, and had been deemed stable enough to travel across the Atlantic. Even though I was completely unconscious for the trip. The doctors now tell me they gave me medicine to make sure I stayed out over the flight. Either way, I don't think it would have been a problem.

When I finally woke up, my first thought was Jenkins. I had to know that he was okay because he's my best friend and pretty much my only friend. They assured me that he was. Apparently, he woke up sometime in Germany and his wife was there for him. They told me that she'd been there for me too and was constantly checking on me for him.

Really, the two of them are the closest thing to family that I have left. Of course, when I woke up, the first thing I tried to do was speak. At first, I thought maybe I couldn't because my throat was dry or maybe I had been intubated and it would just take a few days to get my voice back. Unfortunately, that was not the case.

Even now, I still momentarily forget and try to talk when people speak to me. It happened just today. When I think about the fact that I'll never speak again, my mind goes in a million directions.

What kind of people will want to be friends with me when I can barely communicate with them? Would a woman want to be in a relationship with a man she can't talk to? Sure, every woman says she wants a good listener, but that only goes so far when the man can't communicate back to prove that he was actually listening.

How the hell am I going to have kids? I will never be able to be left alone with them. I won't be able to tell them no don't touch that or don't do that or don't go out there. So what's the point of having kids if I can't be left alone with them? That's not fair to their mother to have all the work for raising them.

This morning I was encouraged to start thinking about what I want to do with my life outside the military so that I had a goal to work towards. I think I looked at the poor woman like she had twelve heads.

What I want to do and what I actually can do with no voice is completely different. What I want is to finish out my time in the military. I had planned to retire from the service, probably at an old age when I was forced to get out.

What I want is a wife and kids, someone to come home to waiting on me instead of an empty house. What I want is a normal life, the kind that I can't have now.

So, what options does that leave me?

Logan

Chapter 4

Faith

I'm having dinner with Lauren and Gavin. Lauren's mom is in town so she has their son, so we can talk about wedding plans tonight. They are getting married on the grounds at Oakside with the beautiful plantation home as their setting.

These two were high school sweethearts, but circumstances separated them. Yet at the same time, it gave them their son. They managed to find their way back to each other only the way true love can.

Gavin lost his sight in the military and shocker of all shockers, Lauren happened to be the one that Oakside brought in to help him out. He's since had surgery but has limited eyesight and is still classified as legally blind. Now he works with Lauren and helps other soldiers at Oakside. Soldiers like Logan's friend, Ken Jenkins.

Not ten minutes after Gavin proposed, Lauren was on the phone with me, asking me to be her maid of honor. Of course I said yes. After college, Lauren and her son lived with me for a while and we became fast friends. I love her son to death and am so happy for Lauren and

Gavin. So, without having to even think about it, my answer was a resounding 'yes.' This dinner is the first real chance we've had to talk about wedding plans. While they're not doing a long engagement and they are having the wedding at Oakside, now it's a matter of just how long it's going to take to get everything put together. Lexi has been using some of her contacts and I am here to get my marching orders.

"I don't want anything too extravagant for my dress. There's a bridal store in Savannah that has a lot of dresses that I'd be able to take home on the same day. One of the girls Lexi knows is going to tailor it for me, so when I have the dress, then we can plan on the wedding date. The chef here at Oakside is going to cook the food. And we're going to invite all the men who are here at Oakside to be part of the wedding.

My parents will be here, as well as a couple of the girls we knew at school. Plus, we'll be inviting some of our friends here," she says, going over a list in the notebook that she brought.

"Are you only having a maid of honor and best man for your wedding party, or will there be more?" I ask. At the same time I'm digging into the chicken parmesan on my plate in front of me. It's been a while since I've been out to eat, but this little Italian place in town is one of my favorites.

"Just you and Graham as best man. Paisley is training Gavin's Seeing Eye dog, Gem, to walk down the aisle with him as the flower girl holding a basket of flower petals in her mouth. Also, she’s taught one of the dogs she has in training to walk down as the ring bearer. That’s the extent of the wedding party."

"Okay, what about clothes for us?"

We spend the next hour going over details, and to his credit, Gavin doesn't once look bored. He simply enjoys the meal and even orders dessert. When asked or when he actually has an opinion on something, he lets us know what he thinks. Like when he told us he wanted to make sure there was kid friendly food for their son at the wedding.

By the time we're done, I feel like we've covered pretty much everything, and assuming we can find her dress when we go down to Savannah, we could have the wedding a lot sooner than either of us really thought possible. That's a good thing, as neither one of them really wanted a big wedding. This is more for show for their son than anything else. But I know Gavin wants to make sure that Lauren has the wedding of her dreams too because it has been a long time coming. I don’t think he would have let her skip out on having a decent wedding and going for something like a courthouse wedding. Something that she had started to talk about. If it came down to it, I'm pretty sure he would have planned the whole wedding himself just to give it to her how he thought it should be.

After going home and sitting at my desk, I stared at the journal that I will be handing off to Logan tomorrow. When I see him, I'm not sure what to write or how deep to get because I'm not sure where his head is at and what he wants to write about.

So, I start with something simple.

Logan,

You're at the beginning of a new journey right now and I know that looking down the road to where you want to end up seems almost impossible, but it's not. Keep in mind that it's not going to happen overnight, and it's going to be a lengthy but gradual progression. So you need to take things slow and have patience with yourself.

You're going to have a lot of people on your team here at Oakside. Lean on us when you need us, as it's what we're here for.

My friend Lauren, who is the one helping your friend Ken is getting married. Her husband Gavin was a patient here at Oakside who also lost his sight. Lexi has offered for them to get married here and they're going to do it as soon as possible. My guess is within the next few months, which means you'll get to be a part of it. You'll get to see that love truly can conquer all and no matter what, there will be people in your corner. It sounds like Ken and his wife are those people for you.

Ken is the one person who knows what you went through and while his injuries are different so your path to healing will be different. He's going to be the closest person to understanding you in this journey. If you can't open up to anyone else, you should at least be able to open up to him.

This journey isn't going to be easy. It's going to be hard and in my experience, there's going to be many times you're going to feel like giving up. But I promise you the reward at the other end is completely worth it. Know this right now, I plan to pull you kicking and screaming if I have to.

Faith

•••••••••••

Even after writing in the journal to Logan last night, I couldn't fall asleep no matter what I did. So, I got up and pulled out Ellie's new cookbook. Ellie and Owen are big donors at Oakside. Not only do they donate a big chunk of money, but they come and volunteer every chance they get along with their kids.

After Lexi told me about her, I picked up her newest cookbook and flipped through it. Since I had bookmarked a lot of recipes, I decided that when I couldn't sleep, I'd get up and make one of the cookie recipes. When they turned out so well, I decided to bring them in when I visit Logan today and use them as a kind of a reward system.

"Good afternoon! I have a snack for you today, but you have to earn it." I tell Logan as I enter the room. Turning to look at me, he raises an eyebrow at my statement, but nothing more.

"First, I want to know if you did your homework," I say. Setting the cookies down, I sign as I speak, and he nods his head.

Hello, my name is Logan. What is your name? Which way to the bathroom?

Even though he signs and while his movements are a bit slow, I can tell he's been practicing them.

"Good job! Before you know it, we'll be having entire conversations in sign language and you won't even think twice about it," I tell him. Then I pick up the tin of cookies, open it, holding them out for him. Looking at me skeptically, he peeks in before picking one up.

"These cookies are from Ellie's new book. Her and her husband are some of Oakside's big donors and will be here for Lauren's wedding," I tell him. Nodding, he takes a bite of the cookie, tasting it, and a huge smile crosses his face.

"Good huh?"

He nods his head enthusiastically and finishes off the cookie in no time.

"It says in your notes that you are clear to walk until you get tired. But it also says you are not to overdo it. How far are you generally able to walk?"

"The furthest I've gone is down to the dining room and back, with no problems." The tablet voice reads out for him.

"You have mastered that very well. So, you haven't been out to the gardens yet?"

He shakes his head no again.

"Alright then, let's get you outside and we can sign the different things along the way. But first, let me teach you how to say 'I need to rest' in case it gets too much for you."

Spending a few minutes until he masters that sign, we then leave, taking our time. As we came across things, I would demonstrate the sign for them. Door. Hallway. Lobby. Desk. Couch. Fireplace. Outside. Porch. Garden.

As we slowly walked through the garden, we'd sign things like flowers, grass and plants. When we saw butterflies or some of the smaller creatures that we'd come across, we would sit down on the garden swing and take a break before going back in.

"We went over a lot today and if only one of the things we learned sticks, then you're doing well. This is going to take time. Tomorrow we'll walk the same path again and go over the same items. Make sure you're watching the videos and hopefully, you wrote in your journal because I wrote in mine." Reaching into my bag, I pull out the journal, holding it out to him. After he takes it, he steps over to the desk and sets it down before picking up his.

He looks at me for just a moment, almost like he's hesitant to give it to me, but then he hands me the journal and I reach taking it from him. Our fingers brush, and for a moment we both stand there looking at the journal and where our hands are touching.

I shouldn't be feeling like this towards a patient. Hell, I don't remember the last time I felt like this at all. Clearing my throat, I move my hand. When he lets go of the journal, I tuck it into my bag and take a step back from him.

"Okay, see you tomorrow. Make sure you do your homework." I tell him, as I slowly back out of the room. His eyes are on me, but his expression is hard to read. So, smiling, I turn around and head out.

When I get home, the first thing I do is pull out Logan's journal and read what he had to say. I know it's not going to be easy. Even though I was prepared for an emotional rollercoaster, what he wrote had me in tears.

Logan,

I will always be here to listen to anything that you need to get out on paper. But let me address a few things. First, I'm really glad you're talking about your accident. It was a very traumatizing experience and I know you will never forget it. I can only imagine the sheer panic you must have felt, and I hope as you work through it in therapy you will find some sense of comfort,

It's wonderful and makes me happy that you have Ken and his wife and consider them family. But I promise you, the people here at Oakside will become your family too. No one ever leaves here completely alone. Going through events like this really bonds you.

But it's going to be up to you, the type of people with which you surround yourself. There are so many people in the world that know sign language, many of which you probably don't even realize. As you start hanging out with people who use sign language or ASL, they'll introduce you to other people. Before long, you'll form a whole new group around you.

Deaf people find the love of their lives, get married and have kids every day. It does take a few extra steps, but you have an advantage in that you can still hear. You'll have to rely on physical activity of getting up and removing your kids from a situation instead of just yelling at them and telling them not to do stuff. But kids will learn ASL as they learn to talk. In fact, many young kids learn signs for certain things before they're even able to form words, so communicating with your kids shouldn't hold you back.

As far as what you want to do, there are many doors open to you. As you become fluent in sign language, there's always the option to teach at a deaf school. Of course, there are always desk jobs, customer service job on the computer via online chats. Or there's always the option of having a translator, if you want to do a job that requires speaking to people,

There are plenty of professions that allow you to work behind the scenes where you only have to speak with a manager with your tablet, which will be pretty easy. When I see you again tomorrow, I'll have a list of ideas ready for you.

You can still have what you call a normal life. Only the process of getting there is going to be a little bit different.

Faith

Chapter 5

Logan

I've now been working with Faith for an entire week. We have a good routine and she's making learning these different words really fun. Since we've been writing back and forth every day in the journals, it's been nice to get to know her and to feel truly seen as she addresses my different concerns and worries.

The problem is, the more I get to know her, the more I want to know her on a completely unprofessional level. One that I'm pretty sure a sweet girl like Faith would not be interested in. Hell, would any girl be interested in getting to know someone who can't even talk? Let's not even mention the scars that I have from the accident. So, I'll just have to settle with spending what time I can with her.

I really like just spending time with her. Daily, I look forward to the energy she brings into the room. A close second is halfway through our walks when we sit down on the swing in the garden. She insists we rest so I don't overdo it per orders from my physical therapist.

While I don't feel like I'm overdoing it or even close to it, but after being bedridden for four months, I guess everyone is just being extra careful with me. I don't protest because I get to sit down and enjoy more time with her.

Right now, we have a few short conversations completely in sign language. So our focus is now on more complete sentences on the things we see on our walks. Instead of saying door, she has me saying the door is open.

Getting to meet with her every day has been the highlight of my day. With the weekend in front of us, I'm definitely not looking forward to it. Which strikes me as odd because in the military, you always looked forward to the weekends and the break to be able to do what you want. Now I don't want the weekends because that means no appointments and basically, other than the nursing staff, I'm kind of on my own to entertain myself. Honestly, I don't want to be alone.

What are you doing this weekend? I sign to her, showing off some of what I have practiced.

"Logan, that's a great job!" She says with a huge smile that lights up her face. That smile right there makes all the practice worth it. "My brother is coming over with his wife to talk about the latest trip they just went on. They got home a few days ago and will probably have a ton of pictures to show off. Then I have some wedding stuff to plan with Lauren. And if I'm lucky, I might have time to read a book that has been sitting on my coffee table for two months now."

Sounds like fun, he signs

"I think it will be. Now, I've been thinking about what I want you to do for your homework and I think it's fairly simple. Though I think it's also going to be pretty hard, but I know you're ready."

Instantly, my nerves kick up. Usually my homework is journaling and videos, and I've been taking it seriously. Yet this sounds like she has something else in store.

What is it? I sign.

"So, I know you go all the time and talk to Ken with the tablet, which is great for both of you. But I think you need to meet some of the other guys and expand your circle. If you can talk to your friend using the tablet, you should talk to people here with it too. Plus, there's the added benefit that many of the men have the same emotions and thoughts that you do, and they could all use a friend."

Even though I know she's right, the thought of putting myself out there to try to make new friends right now is more than just terrifying. It makes me physically sick. I'm trying really hard not to think about it, but I know that she'll push me to do it.

On the way back in, she points out a few of the guys that are sitting out on the front porch. I just smile and nod and listen to what she has to say.

By the time we get back up to my room, the same thought keeps swirling in my head. I don't really want to go talk to anyone new. Even more, I wish that she was going to be around for me to talk to.

"You look sad. What's wrong?" she asks when we get to my room.

Shaking my head, I try to brush it off, but she gives me a look that says she knows something is wrong and she isn't going to give up until I tell her.

Again, fighting the urge to roll my eyes, I grab my tablet. She's patient as I type, waiting for the tablet to start speaking.

"I was just getting used to you being here and my team of doctors and the nurses. Now I have to go back to an entire weekend of being alone and I'm not looking forward to it."

"Okay, I understand. Give me a moment to talk to Noah. I have an idea, but I have to get approval first"

I nod interested to see what her idea is and watch her walk out the door. But I don't have to wait long because she comes back with a huge smile on her face.

"All right, I got permission for you to use social media on your tablet." She holds her hand out for my tablet and I give it to her. As she starts poking away, she continues to talk.

"I suggest you use it to join groups and meet people that might be like you. That will give you a chance to connect with others. If you go ahead and either log into your account or create an account, I'll have you send me a friend request and we can chat throughout the weekend whenever you need to talk to someone."

Then she hands me back the tablet open to a social media account that I haven't used in forever. I type in my details and thankfully, with one try, I get the password correct and it logs me right in. Handing it back to her, she pokes around in silence for a few minutes before giving it back to me.

"That's my account. When I get home, I will accept your friend request and then I'm there if you need someone to talk to. Noah should be by later and he said that he would be happy to add you on there as well so you can message him. When Easton and Jake come by, you can connect with them, too. That should give you plenty of people to chat with while you're making new friends with the guys that are here."

Thank you, I sign.

I'm way more excited than I should be that I will still be able to connect with her over the weekend. But I'm not going to let on about that fact. Though she did just open the door for me to be able to connect with people on a whole another level, which is great. She is right. I'm sure there are plenty of groups out there that will allow me to connect with people and get some advice and tips.

Before she leaves, she pulls the journal out of her bag and hands it to me. Like we've done previously, I pick up the one that's on the desk and hand it to her. It's our normal exchange every time before she leaves.

And like every other day, I watch her go and then wait about ten minutes before I open up the journal to see what she wrote me back.

Logan,

I want you to know how truly proud I am of how seriously you're taking watching the videos at night and doing the homework. You're moving at an amazing pace even though I'm sure to you it doesn't feel like it. You have to remember you're learning an entirely new language and it doesn't happen overnight.

Before I left today, I had a conversation with Lexi, and she said that it excited a lot of the staff to learn some of the basic ASL so that they can talk to you, too. People from the kitchen and even some of the volunteers want to learn. It's really heartwarming how the people around here have rallied to support you, and I hope it makes you feel less alone.

By the way, I watched that TV show you recommended, and I toughed it out past the first episode, which you were right, was really gory. But I'm on episode three and I'm hooked, so if I don't get all my extra work finished, just know that it's all your fault.

I apologize for this journal entry being shorter, but my sister-in-law called, and we were talking for a while and now it is time for me to go to bed because it's really late.

You'll be reading this going into the weekend, so just know that I am going to miss seeing what you have to say each day. This has become one of my favorite parts of my nighttime routine, and I look forward to it each night.

See you on Monday.
Faith

This letter is much shorter than the others. Just the other day, I had asked her how she got in this line of work. She was talking about her time at school and doing different clinical rotations until she landed at the hospital and saw someone struggling to communicate.

At that point, she only knew a little sign language, but she was able to help him and the sense of accomplishment she felt was something she wanted for the rest of her life.

I've learned that she is one of the most kind and generous people you will ever meet, and she will help someone without expecting anything in return.

After I decide to write her a letter each day over the weekend, I grab a pen and start with today.

Faith

I'm glad you and your sister-in-law get on so well. How did you and your brother get along growing up? I'm guessing as the older brother, he had a lot of work keeping the guys in line around you. It might be a bit inappropriate to say, but you are absolutely beautiful and with such a kind soul there probably was a long line of guys wanting to bask in your attention.

Your poor brother probably couldn't keep up. If you're going to tell me that it's not true, and that your brother didn't have to fend off any of the guys, I suggest you have a serious talk with him. Because he's either lying to you or shielding you from the truth, or you just never realized it until now.

I never had any siblings. In a way, I think it was a blessing, as I don't think my grandparents could have handled more than one of me at a time. I was quite a handful growing up and I definitely would have been one of the guys your brother would have wanted to keep away from you.

I'm pretty sure it's why my grandfather had many long talks on the porch with me about joining the Army. Then because I couldn't do as he wanted, I went and joined the Navy to become a Navy pilot. My grandfather, being an Army vet, was still at my boot camp graduation and extremely proud of me. Even though he still wore army stuff most of the time, every now and then he'd sneak in a Navy hat or a Navy T-shirt which just tickled me to death after all the shit he used to talk about the navy growing up.

Each day this weekend, I'm going to write you a letter. I'm not sure what about. But I'm sure I'll have plenty to talk about. In the meantime, I look forward to hearing how your weekend went with your brother and with all the wedding planning.

Logan.

Chapter 6

Faith

I'm sitting in my living room talking with my brother and sister-in-law about their last trip to Mexico. They've been married almost two years and have been traveling every couple of months. They like to joke and say it's an extended honeymoon.

Both their jobs are remote work from home jobs, so it's pretty easy for them to pack up and go whenever they feel like it. This time, they traveled around Mexico for just shy of three weeks. They did some hiking and visited some historical sites including the Mayan pyramids which have always been big on my brother's list of things to see.

"So, you started seeing a new patient at Oakside while we were gone, didn't you?" my brother asks.

We weren't always super close growing up, but now that we're older, we've gotten closer. Since he got married, we make it a point to get together for dinner at least once a month if not more.

"Yeah, I absolutely love Oakside. It's got all the history of an old plantation home, but it feels absolutely cozy.

Even with all the people there, you could still crawl up on a couch in the lobby to read a book by the fireplace. The owners, Noah and Lexi, are some of the nicest people you will ever meet. With each patient, they're truly involved with their care, making sure they have everything they could need or want."

"Tell us what you can about your patient," Dawn, my brother's wife, says.

I had to stop myself from cringing when she refers to Logan as my patient. But that's what he is, isn't he? It's been only a week and somewhere along the line I've been thinking of him as more of a friend I'm helping out than a person I'm getting paid to help.

That's a very dangerous line to cross. It may have worked out for Lauren, but she had dated Gavin in high school, so the situation was completely different.

"He was a Navy pilot, and his plane went down him. Both he and his copilot were both injured. Unfortunately, he lost his voice and his copilot lost his sight," I tell them. Then realize I probably have told them a little too much and think it has to do with the fact that the lines are really blurred between Logan and me right now. I need to make sure that I take care of that come Monday.

"How's he doing so far?" my brother Eddy asks.

"Good for basically having to learn a whole new language. Apparently, the copilot who was on the plane that lost his sight is his best friend, so he's been learning and using the tablet to communicate with him. Everything he needs to learn will take time. He's good at doing the homework I assigned him so he's picking it up pretty fast. Now enough of that, tell me more about this trip," I say, trying to switch the subject. Dawn looks over at my brother and they seem to have a silent conversation before she nods her head.

"Well," my brother says, "you know they say don't drink the water in Mexico and they say it for a reason. Towards the end of the trip, Dawn started feeling really sick, and we spent a few days being lazy in our room. We were hoping she would feel better before we had to come home."

"Oh no, how are you feeling? You look like you're doing well now. I would have never known you were sick," I say.

"Well, I was able to get an appointment the day after we got home. Even though I was starting to feel better, I went anyway. Well, as it turns out, you're going to be an aunt," she says. Looking at me, they both freeze, waiting for my reaction.

It took a moment for what she said to really sink in. During that time, neither my brother nor Dawn moved an inch.

"Wait, you're pregnant?" I ask, still trying to process the information.

She nods with a delighted smile on her face, and I jump up, running over to give her a hug.

"I can't believe I'm finally going to have a little niece or nephew running around. Just you wait. I'm going to spoil him or her so good they're going to want to be at Auntie Faith's house all the time."

At my words, they laugh and look delighted. Then they start talking about their doctor's appointment. When my phone goes off, I glance at it and find that it's Logan. He's on messenger telling me that he spent the morning with Ken, and they went for a walk in the garden. Though he knows I'm not a new person like I wanted him to talk to, but he wanted me to know he wasn't just sitting in his room.

As my brother and Dawn keep talking about this and that for the baby, they interject and ask my opinion now and then. All the while, I keep texting back and forth with Logan.

"Who are you talking to?" my brother asks in a playful tone.

"Oh, it's just that patient I was telling you about." When I tried to blow it off, my brother was not having it.

"With the smile he's putting on your face, I'd say he's much more than a patient."

Whoops. I didn't realize I was smiling until just now when my brother pointed it out. But I am and my cheeks hurt because of it. Just for this little bit, I enjoyed talking to Logan, and I definitely miss seeing him today.

"It's not like that and it's definitely not going anywhere. This is the guy I was telling you about who lost his voice in the plane crash." I'm hoping to offer them just enough information that they'll drop it. Of course, this is my brother, so I should have known better.

"Oh, it's definitely going somewhere. You don't smile like that for nothing. Come on, we need to know more about this guy," Dawn chimes in.

"There is nothing to tell, but if there is, I promise I will let you know," I tell them. But my brother still stares at me with an expression on his face I can't quite make out. Dawn looks over and elbows him. Then he finally looks away and his face relaxes slightly.

Logan: So, they're doing a movie on the lawn which pretty much everyone is going to. The problem is, it's some black and white film I really don't want to sit through. Let's play a fun version of twenty questions, so I don't go out of my mind with boredom.

Me: My brother and sister-in-law are still here, but I will play. Though I might be a bit slow in responding.

Logan: I'll take it. If you could live anywhere, where would it be and why?

Me: Starting right the gate with a double question? I'll let it go just this once. I'd live in the Beartooth Mountains just outside Yellowstone National Park. Once I went there on vacation, and it was the most beautiful and peaceful place I've ever been. Now the same question back to you.

All night we continued finding out each other's favorite foods and favorite childhood memories, including things we disliked. One we both agreed on was our hate for Brussels sprouts.

I find out Logan loves to garden and that he hasn't had a good home cooked meal since his grandmother died several years ago.

While trying to be respectful answering the texts and giving my brother and sister-in-law the attention they deserve, it's a delicate balance. When I do answer the texts, they don't want to call me out on it. Later that night, as they're getting ready to leave, my brother pulls me off to the side.

"I really like seeing you happy. This kind of reminds me of how I used to feel when I was getting to know Dawn," he says with a dreamy look on his face. That man is head over heels in love with his wife. No one who spends any amount of time around them could deny it. Since he's my brother, I try to be honest and open with him.

"The man who writes in the journals that we trade back every day, is a man who is stealing my heart and it terrifies me."

"What about the man you work with every day in person?"

"Sometimes it's hard to reconcile the two and know they're the same person. But he's well on the way to stealing my heart, too. Though I keep fighting it because he's my patient. Ultimately, I don't know if I'm going to win the fight."

"Then make sure you talk to Lexi about it. Keep it professional or they might have to assign someone else to him. Especially if you decide you want to see if it can go anywhere. Which for the record, I absolutely think you should based on how happy you are tonight." My brother then gives me a huge hug before he helps his wife in to his truck.

As they get ready to leave, I watch them. He opens her door, makes sure she's settled before moving to his side of the vehicle. I don't know where my brother got his manners because it sure as hell wasn't from our parents.

Going to my office, I pull out the journal that we've been passing back and forth. I know it's about to be lights out there at Oakside and that just means everyone needs to go back to their rooms. Even though they should go to bed, the staff doesn't force people to go to sleep. There are so many there who can't sleep. Texting Logan, I tell him that my brother left and that I'm probably heading to bed soon. I say goodnight and tells me he's going to bed too.

Feeling restless, I get up and check the house, making sure everything's locked, all the lights are turned off, and everything's cleaned up. Then I go to my office, sit down and read Logan's past entries in the journal before writing him another one.

Logan,

At dinner tonight, my brother told me that he and his wife are pregnant. This is the first baby in our family in a really long time. The look of pure joy on his face and my sister-in-law's face at that moment is something I know I'll never forget.

Growing up, I didn't have a good example of true love. I assume my mother and father love each other, but they just never really showed it. Seeing my brother and his wife, Dawn together, I'm beginning to understand what it really is. I know that a child is going to be brought up in a home full of love because my brother wouldn't allow anything less and neither will I.

They told me first and still have to go tell my sister-in-law's family. I love having this little secret between us. Even though I know that you grew up with your grandparents and we never really talk too much about the details with our parents, I'll tell you a little of my story because, for whatever reason, it's fresh in my mind tonight.

My mom was pregnant with my brother in college, and they were forced to get married. During that time, old southern families still had shotgun weddings. I'm sure my parents have respect for each other and they are still together to this day, but if I saw them on the street I would never use the word love to describe them.

They work hard, and work well together, but they are more like friends who are raising a family together than anything else.

At one point, my brother told me that he remembers my parents fighting when my mom became pregnant with me. My dad felt that Mom had planned it. I never felt anything but love from both my parents, but I don't think either my brother or I were planned at all.

Now that we are on our own, they are traveling all over the place. She's happier than we've ever seen her and she's in great shape because they do some pretty outrageous hikes. Even if they won't admit it, I'm pretty sure they're training to climb Mount Everest.

They will be back in town in a few weeks. My brother has decided to tell them in person about the baby. I'm actually really excited about helping plan the reveal.

So, that's the long ramble of my family story. We're not all perfect, but I think our life is what we make of it.

Faith

Chapter 7

Logan

I will give Oakside credit for trying to make weekends fun. They have all sorts of different activities and things to do and movies every night. Though I still have yet to do the homework that Faith asked me to do, and I know I'm running out of time. It's not my intention to disappoint her, but I am dragging my feet. When Noah walks in, I'm trying to talk myself into joining whatever event is going on in the dining hall.

"Hey man, I thought I'd come and check on you. Maybe we can work on some of these sign language videos together. Do you have time?" he asks, standing by my door. When I nod, he smiles, entering and sitting on the couch with me.

He has his own tablet in his hands and pulls up whatever video he was looking at and we pick up practicing right where he left off. Actually, I enjoy practicing with someone else because I don't feel like the only idiot making some of these hand motions. After getting some good laughs in, Noah switches to some sports videos, and we learn how to talk sports.

Today, it was great working with Noah while we practiced with these videos. It made things so much easier.

"Alright, let's head down for dinner. Maybe afterward you'll join us for game night." At Noah's words, a pit forms in my stomach.

Game Night will be the last chance to do the homework Faith gave me, so I don't have a choice but to follow Noah out of the room and downstairs to the dining room.

"Each Sunday we try to make a home-style meal. Something that would make you feel like it came from your mom or your grandma's kitchen. It's the one day we loosen all the healthy food requirements and have things like chocolate cake for dessert. At the end of the weekend, before the start of another long week, it gives everyone something to look forward to," Noah says. After handing me a tray, he's patient with me about helping me get my food. Before long, the person serving me is not understanding what I want. But then, one guy at the other end of the counter sees me, smiles and runs up to take the girl's place who was getting frustrated.

I've been practicing, he signs with a big grin.

Noah takes my tray for me so I can use my hands.

So have I. I really appreciate it, I tell him.

With a big smile on his face, he walks with me through the line to help me get my food and then Noah and I go to a table where there are a couple other guys and a woman sitting beside them.

"Okay, introductions. This grumpy bearded fellow is Easton, and the bubbly ray of sunshine beside him is his wife Paisley. Easton is a former patient and now is our head of security. Paisley helps train any of the service dogs that we need for the men and women here at Oakside. This beautiful girl on Easton's side is Ali, his service dog. You'll see her with him at all times.

This couple here who can't seem to keep their hands off of themselves are Mandy and Levi. They are newly married. Levi is also a former patient and Mandy is one of our office workers. She helps with the charity funding budgeting and a little bit of everything at this point. Levi works with security, helping with many of the events here, like tonight's Game Night.

This is Jake. He was not a patient here, but he is former military and also has one of Paisley's service dogs. The big guy beside him is Atticus, and he also helps volunteer here with security and events.

Before anyone asks, Lexi is helping with wedding planning and is with Lauren and Faith. Everyone, this is Logan, the guy I've been telling you about," Noah says, finally sitting down.

After the introductions, everyone is nice, and they include me in the conversation as if I've always just been part of the group.

"Noah, what's it like having the new baby at home?" Jake asks.

Noah's face lights up brighter than a Christmas tree at midnight. He doesn't even have to answer the question because that face says it all.

"It's crazy to think that I get to be responsible for another human being. I love every minute of it, but it's not easy. The worst is the sleepless nights trying to figure out what's wrong when you have no clue, but I wouldn't change it for the world. What about you guys? How's married life treating you?" he asks Levi and Mandy.

They look at each other with happy smiles on their faces.

"Really great! The best part is Rebecca is finally starting to come around now that she sees how truly happy we really are." Mandy says, turning to me.

"Rebecca is my best friend. She dated Levi in high school, but they broke up when he joined the military. I had no idea he was here until we crossed paths one night and one thing led to another. Though I never set out to date my best friend's ex-boyfriend, it's kind of in the girl's handbook of something you don't do. To put it mildly, she was not happy. But thankfully she's coming around. Rebecca and her husband have some things to work through because he was not quite as understanding, but that's for them to deal with."

Even though she smiles, I can tell there's some concern there for her best friend, too.

Once we're done eating, Noah takes me out to the back porch where game night is being held. Obviously, they're taking advantage of the absolutely beautiful weather.

"So, there are some card games going on over there. I'd be happy to be your partner," Jake says, walking beside me.

I just nod and follow them over.

"Good luck and have fun," Noah says, going back inside.

"This is Shane and Mike." Jake introduces us and we sit down to play some cards.

Time seems to fly by as we joke around and play several rounds. Then on my way back up to my room, Noah stops me again.

"You look like you were having fun out there."

I really was.

"Good. It wasn't so bad to complete your homework now, was it?" he says with a smile.

You knew?

"Of course, I did. Faith asked me to make sure that you got out and met someone new this weekend."

Shaking my head, I go upstairs to my room. After I get ready for bed, I sit down at the desk to write Faith another letter in the journal.

Faith,

With Noah's help, I completed your homework assignment. He came in today and we practiced some of the sign language videos, including some on sports. Then we went to dinner together. He introduced me to Mandy and

Levi, Easton and Paisley, and Jake. We all had dinner together.

After dinner, the Game Night was out on the back patio, where Jake introduced me to Shane and Mike. We played cards for a good part of the evening. It wasn't so bad, and everyone has been really patient. Though I know that won't be the norm in my everyday life because people here understand we served and were injured. Not everyone in the outside world will be patient and encouraging. That's what I really truly dread.

I also know by telling you this, you're going to find some way of making me face my fear. With whatever plan you have, just please make sure that you're there with me when I'm doing it for the first time. Having some support around me makes it much easier.

I can't wait to see you tomorrow. Since I have PT in the morning, I know it's going to seem like forever. In any case, I really look forward to our walks in the garden.

Logan

Chapter 8

Faith

All weekend I have been looking forward to the drive down the long oak lined driveway to Oakside. Not just to see Logan, even though that's a big part of it, but because for some reason it's like a portal into another time. All my troubles stay at the road, and it allows me to focus on Logan without the outside world slipping in. I wonder if the guys here feel like that too. As if they can heal without the influence of the outside world.

I'll have to ask Logan. Because if that is how he's feeling, I need to make sure that we do some practice out in town so that he's truly ready for the transition.

Sitting in my car, I take a few deep breaths, trying to calm my nerves before heading in to see Logan. After leaving my car, I decided to take the long way inside going through the side door that leads to the downstairs offices. Seeing Noah in his office that he shares with his wife, I knock on the door, getting his attention.

"I was hoping I'd run into you. When you were here on Sunday with Logan, I wanted to see how it went."

"Actually, I think he's doing really well, considering he has some anxiety when it comes to putting himself out there and meeting new people. But honestly, take a look around. You can't throw a stone without hitting a guy that doesn't have anxiety about meeting someone new in their current condition. Around here, it's a side effect of being injured."

"I know, but it's my job to push him outside of his comfort zone. On the way here, I was thinking I need to get him outside of Oakside and functioning in everyday scenarios. Of course, whenever he gets the approval from his doctors."

"Though I'll mention it to his doctors, I think it will still be awhile before he'll be ready to leave the grounds and go out in public. He's just beginning PT, and they will need to assess him and see what he is able to do. Being bedridden for several months can take its toll on the body in ways you really wouldn't expect."

"I figured, but just let me know." With that, I make my way upstairs and to his room.

The weather was so nice I'm already looking forward to our walk in the garden. But the sight that greets me when I walk into his room almost breaks my heart. Lying in bed alone in the quiet room, he looks absolutely miserable.

"Logan?" I ask, stepping into the room. When he looked at me, I'm pretty sure if he could have made a sound, he would have groaned.

"What's wrong? Do you need me to get your nurse?" I ask.

No. Over did it at PT. Just really sore, he signs.

"Well, we can switch gears and have some lessons here. You don't even have to get out of bed. Does your nurse at least know how you're feeling?"

He nods his head yes, so I grab the remote for the TV and turn it on, looking for a show that's educational and would make for a great lesson.

Finally, I find a home restoration show. Even though it sounds crazy, there are many common everyday terms and uses in it that makes for a great lesson. From where he is in bed, he can easily see the TV. So, I position myself at the end of the bed so he can still see the TV, but he'll be able to see me signing as well. He turns carefully so he has a better view and I start signing what is being said on TV.

After getting through two of the shows, I can tell his concentration is starting to wane, so I turn the TV off. Then I grab his tablet off the coffee table and bring it to him.

"What did you do to injure yourself?" I ask.

He takes the tablet and starts typing on it while I wait patiently for him to answer my question.

"We were doing some exercises, and the PT told me to do as any many reps as I could, and I pushed myself. I thought..." he turns the tablet off mid-sentence and shakes his head.

"You thought what? You know you can tell me anything, right?"

He shakes his head again, but I don't give up. Staring at him, I raise my eyebrow, letting him know I want to know. Finally, he sighs and turns back to the tablet and starts typing again.

"I thought if I could do more, I would be done faster. Then we could go on longer walks and do more."

"You feel stuck where you are?" I ask reading between the lines.

Yes.

"Healing is a journey and not an easy one at that. Your mind might be ready for the next step, but your body isn't. There will be times when your body is ready for the next step, but your mind isn't. Every person in this building has been there, and I guarantee you that you weren't the only one thinking if you push yourself a little bit more you'd heal faster. But that's not the case. When you push yourself like this, you're setting yourself back."

That's what he said to me.

"Then maybe you should listen to him." I smile, trying to keep it playful even though I mean every word that I say.

Can we watch some TV just for fun now?

After checking my watch, we still have time before our dinner, so I agree and hand him the TV remote. I'm curious to see what he is going to pick and am relieved when he picks a comedy.

At one part during the movie I'm laughing, and I can feel his body shaking next to me. When I look over, he has the biggest smile on his face. At this moment, I can't take my eyes off of him. He seems so carefree, and it makes me wish that I could give him more of this.

When he stops laughing, he must sense my eyes on him because with a smile on his face, he turns to look at me. Both of us stare at each other, neither of us saying a word. The tension in the air is thick between us, but neither of us pulls away.

My heart is racing with the way he is looking at me, and with how close his body is to mine. So close, I can feel his body heat. Is he getting closer or is that my imagination? I'm pretty sure he's leaning into me. Is he going to kiss me?

Looking at his lips, they are lips I'd love nothing more than to feel on mine. I run my tongue along my mouth as if I can already feel the loss of his lips. Hesitantly, he reaches up and tucks a strand of hair behind my ear but leaves his hand on the side of my face, like he's testing if I'm going to push him away. Of course I'm not.

When I lean into him, his hand goes behind my head and pulls me the rest of the way until our lips are touching. This kiss is unlike anything I've ever experienced in my life. It's as if our souls are connecting, not just our lips.

Turning his body toward mine, he deepens the kiss. I can't deny that I'm drawn to him in a powerful, primal way. My body is telling me the closer I get to him, the better the kiss will be. Forget that this is already the best kiss of my life or how turned on I am from this kiss alone. My body wants more, and I want more.

Just as I'm about to push forward and take what I want, a noise in the hallways reminds me of where we are. Anyone could walk in and see us. Not to mention this is the last thing I should be doing with a patient. It's completely unprofessional even if I want it.

"We... umm... probably shouldn't do that again," I stumble over my words, getting out of bed.

But I want to do it again. With all my heart.

Standing there, I stare at him and know I need to get moving and put this behind us before I end up back in his bed for a different reason.

I pull the journal out of my bag and set it on the coffee table for him.

On the desk is the one for you, he signs.

Grabbing the journal off the desk, I get my stuff determined to get out of there and go home to sort through my feelings. I rush through our goodbyes and pray I don't run into anyone on the way out. Fate seems to be on my side because I don't and make it to my car.

Taking a deep breath, I try to recenter myself before I drive home. But in my head, I'm already drafting what I want to say to him and I haven't even read his letter yet.

Logan

I shouldn't want to kiss you again. It's highly unprofessional. I shouldn't want you the way that I do because it could backfire for both of us.

But I can't stop these feelings no matter how much I try. I can't act on them because I came here with the goal to help you get better, to help you learn to navigate the world. I need to focus on that goal and follow through. Taking us anything beyond a professional relationship would be a bad idea.

But damn it. That doesn't mean I don't want to.

Faith

Chapter 9

Logan

I can't wait for Faith to get here today. After our kiss yesterday, I'm looking forward to her being here even more. That kiss was life changing. It's the kind you see described in books and movies, but don't think actually exists. Well, it does exist because I just experienced it last night.

After resting yesterday, I'm feeling better but my physical therapist is insisting I take a couple of days off before getting back to it. He gave me the same speech Faith did that I was not helping myself, but was hurting myself by pushing that hard.

Today I have to see my regular doctor and the therapist and then I pretty much have a free day other than seeing Faith. As I'm walking downstairs to one of my appointments, I run into Noah in the hallway.

"Hey man, you have a pretty big smile on your face for someone who just overdid it in physical therapy. I'm glad today is a much better day."

Thank you. I'm going for my doctor's appointment.

"Well, I'm heading that way too, so let me walk with you," he says.

I nod, waiting for him to finish talking to the nurse before we go downstairs.

"So, are you going to let me in on the secret of what has you so happy?" he asks as we enter the elevator.

I shake my head. I'm not ready to share it yet and I'm not sure if she even wants me to.

"Okay, well, whenever you are ready, I would love to know because I'm always looking to motivate the other guys here, so if you've found a good motivation tool, let me know," he says.

We exit the elevator, cross the lobby into the hallway that takes us to the dining room, the library and most of the doctor's offices.

"Well, this is where I leave you. We're having another game night this weekend and I hope you'll join us. It was really great seeing you out and spending time with the guys."

Saying goodbye, I head to my doctor's appointment where he basically gives me a once over to make sure I didn't do anything worse when I overdid it at PT. But since I'm feeling much better this morning, it's really a courtesy exam and another lecture of how overdoing it doesn't actually help. During his lecture, I fight the urge to roll my eyes.

After that, I meet with my therapist before grabbing a snack and going into the lobby. Faith should be here at any time. Then I look up, and there she is in the lobby. Our eyes lock and for a moment, it's just us.

That goofy smile I've been fighting all day returns and her face lights up when she sees it.

You ready for our walk? she signs.

I nod. I'm more than ready to get outside.

As we walk, she has me go over detailed descriptions of all the items. We pass from the front door to the front porch, the walkway and into the garden and finally, we're sitting down on the bench when she finally speaks.

"Once you're cleared to go back to PT, we'll switch up our path and go to the barn. Even though it's a longer walk, I think once you've had time to heal, you can handle it."

I'd like that. Why do they have a barn? I ask because I haven't heard much about it.

"They just brought in some horses to do some equine therapy. It's all about learning to trust again and building that relationship with the horse. Really, it's important and helpful to get you to learn how to trust yourself again. Also, helping with a lot of the barn work is another great way for the men and women learning how to get around with the prosthetic are able to practice using it.

On top of that, it teaches skills they can then use out in the civilian world to help get a job. Ranch hands are in high demand, and it doesn't require a lot of people skills."

Sitting here with her like this, there's nothing more I want to do than to kiss her again.

She turns, catching me watching her looking at her lips and hopefully, is remembering the feel of them on mine.

"Logan, we can't. Especially not out here." She says looking around and I get the point. It's a very public space.

Let's head inside. I say.

She agrees, and as we stand up, there's gravel under our feet and she slips. Reaching out, I help steady her, resting my hands on her hips. She grabs hold of my shirt to try to stop the fall. Can we at least just hold each other up?

Having this woman in my arms it's something I know I won't ever forget. She fits completely like she was always meant to be with me. But then I get a feeling she's putting walls up and wonder if she even wants this. The need to kiss her is so acute that it's all I can do not to act on it. But before I kiss her, she takes a deep breath and steps back.

"Sorry, I'm not usually this clumsy," she says.

I reluctantly drop my hands. *It's ok. I really don't mind*, I say.

Even though that seems to shake her a bit, she turns to go back inside. I follow her, but neither one of us says anything until we get up to my room, where she closes the door behind us.

Not waiting for her to speak, I wrap my arm around her waist, pulling her into me. Then I give her the kiss I've been waiting for all day. My lips are on hers and suddenly, everything seems right again. She melts into me, wrapping her arms around my neck. If it's even possible, this kiss is even better than the last.

Never have I been this into kissing. For me, it was always a lead into something else, something more. But with this girl in my arms, I feel like I could sit here and kiss her all night and not be bored, not have the need for more. Sliding my hands into her hair, I gently tilt her head back and glide my mouth down her neck, wanting to taste all of her.

"Logan, no, we can't," she moans, pushing herself off of me.

Why not?

"Because you're my patient, and we can't do this. We... just can't," she sounds like she's trying to convince herself instead of me.

After taking a few steps back, she goes to her bag and pulls out the journal that we've been swapping. I take a deep breath, trying to get myself to relax, and then go to the desk, grabbing the journal for her.

While I don't want to push her, especially if she's not ready, but I'm not backing down either. She takes the journal for me and hands it to me and takes the one that I wrote in, and then she gets her stuff and leaves. It's obvious that she's running scared from something. I'm just not sure what but it's clear as day. Though she knows better than anyone what she's getting herself into with me, and if she's willing to take me as I am, then I'm willing to wait a lifetime for her.

After she leaves, I go to the desk and read what she wrote to me. When there's a soft knock on the door, I look up and find Noah standing there.

"I figured it out," he says to me with a smile. But the smile doesn't quite reach his eyes.

Figured what out? I write with my tablet.

"The smile you had earlier. It was the same one that I had when things started moving with Lexi. I figured it was a relationship of some kind. Until I saw Faith leave just now, I didn't put together who it was."

I cringe because I'm sure based on her reaction that this is the last thing that she wants for Noah to know. Feeling like I need to protect her, while at the same time, not putting her job at risk either.

I like her a lot. Even though right now she's keeping me at arm's length, I can wait because I'm a patient man.

Noah doesn't need to know everything, but letting him know that Faith has integrity and takes her job seriously will hopefully put an end to this. After all, the last thing I want is to get her fired.

"Listen, I get it. A good woman can heal all wounds. You won't be the first one, and I doubt you'll be the last. Any woman who can deal with all our bullshit here, is special and to be treasured. We've had more than our fair share of matches here at Oakside. The problem is walking that professional line and that's something with which she's going to struggle. Also, it's something that Lexi and I because we are in charge of your care, have to watch. So just be careful, okay?" he says.

I nod because I get what he's saying.

As soon as he leaves, I read what Faith wrote. When I read about how much she likes me and how much she shouldn't, it only confirms my belief even more. She wants an 'us.' I could feel it in her kiss, but she's scared of losing her job. While I can't blame her for that, I need to find a way to prove to her we are worth the risk. Never have I been more certain of anything in my life.\

Faith

I understand you're scared, and I understand why. So, I'm not going to push you into something that you weren't completely ready for, but I'm also not going anywhere. Right now, I have nothing but time and am perfectly content using that time to wait on you until you're ready for us.

Take time to get used to the idea. For now, let's just get to know each other. Even though we've been doing that, let's make a conscious effort to get to really know each other. Hopefully, that'll make your choice easier whichever direction you decide if there is one. If that's what you truly want, I'll respect it.

What I don't want is for you to make a knee jerk reaction based on what you think you should or shouldn't do. So let's just go slow.

Logan

Chapter 10

Faith

Every day on my way to Oakside, I get butterflies in my belly. It's been like this for weeks. Well, two weeks and three days to be exact. Ever since that first kiss with Logan. I agreed to take things slow and to get to know him, but that hasn't stopped him from finding ways to sneak in a kiss at least once a day.

It's always different and never predictable. I find it's part of the fun. Even though I shouldn't want it, I desperately do. Today, I got here a little early to talk to Lexi. I figure at the very least she deserves a heads up of what's going on. Then maybe she can give me some insight.

I know nurse Brooke met her husband Luke while he was a patient here and I know Lauren reconnected with Gavin here while he was a patient. Granted, Lauren and Gavin had a history and knew each other from when they were really young, but it still fell under the patient and provider category.

So I know it's not automatic that I would lose my job, but I feel like I owe them at least an explanation. I just don't feel right keeping them in the dark anymore.

When I find Lexi, she's at the front desk, completely overwhelmed with a crying baby and trying to talk to a family member.

Rushing to her side, I take the baby from her.

"Here, I have him. We're going to go hang out in the lobby, so take your time," I tell her.

Giving the family member an apologetic smile, she says to me, "Thank you. He just ate so he shouldn't be hungry, but his bag is behind the desk."

After grabbing his bag, I get comfortable on one of the oversized couches in the lobby.

First off, I check his diaper. He's good to go in that department, so I figure if she just got done feeding him, it might be gas. Sitting down, I pat his back, soothing him, until he stops crying.

I've always been good with kids. When Lauren and her son lived with me for a little bit after college, I learned a lot. For a brief time, I considered going into Pediatrics in some capacity, so I did a lot of rotations in the childrens' units in school.

Once he's calmed down, I start playing to keep him occupied. Since he doesn't seem overly tired, just keeping him happy is the goal at the moment. So, I bounce him around on my knee and make silly faces at him to keep him entertained while his mom is busy.

As I sit here and probably make a fool out of myself for him, it doesn't take long before he has a big old smile on his face. But I don't care. As long as he's happy and Lexi can finish what she needs to do, I'm fine. Most people pass by and smile at us, but in the corner of my eye, I can tell someone has walked up and stopped. When I look up, I find Logan and he's just staring at us.

"You can sit down with us. I'm just watching him until Lexi's done talking to a family member." I give him a smile.

Only he doesn't move. He continues to stand there for a moment before shaking his head and then lifts his hands.

I can't ever give that to you, he signs.

There's a look of pure heartbreak on his face and I'm not quite sure what's running through his head. One thing I do know is out here in the open for everyone to see and hear is not the place to talk about it.

"Can we talk when I'm done here?" I ask him to sign because my hands are busy with the baby.

Instead, he nods, but his expression is still unchanging.

"Okay, I'll meet you in your room. Go on up and write down what you're feeling. I'm not sure how long it'll be, but I will meet you there as soon as I can," I tell him.

After nodding again, he stays for a moment longer before walking off.

Though I try to focus on the baby, my mind is elsewhere. Before I know it, Lexi flops down on the couch beside me.

"Thank you so much for taking him. He's starting to get a lot more vocal and sleep a lot less," she says, taking her son from me.

"I hate to say it because I know how hands on you and Noah want to be, but it might be time to look into getting a nanny. It doesn't have to be someone who stays home with the baby. You can have one who follows you around here at Oakside, but is able to take your son like I did. They could bring him over here to the couch when you have to talk to a family member or help keep him entertained as needed. If you have a phone call or things like that, they could take him for walks in the garden. You know you're both so busy with this place that having an extra set of hands to help out is not going to be a bad thing."

"I know! Especially after today, it proves to me that it's definitely needed. I'll talk to Noah tonight." She smiles at her son.

"One more thing. Is there some place we can duck in for a bit of privacy on something?" I ask.

The smile drops from her face. "Yeah, come to the office beside the lobby. It's empty at the moment." She picks up her son and his bag and leads the way as I follow.

This is the office used for doctors when they're visiting or any other specialty staff that needs to use it, such as myself. I just haven't had a reason to use it.

"Is everything okay?" she asks the moment the door closes.

"I hope so. I just wanted to bring something to your attention because I feel like you have the right to know. But I don't want this to affect us or the care that I'm giving in any way, but Logan and I kissed," I tell her. Then hold my breath, waiting for her reaction.

She looks at me, studying me to see if I have anything else to say, but her reaction is slow.

"What about feelings? Because a kiss is one thing, but when feelings get involved it's another," she says.

"I don't know. I do like him and if it was any other circumstance, I wouldn't even think twice about dating him. But I understand he's my patient. He's admitted that he likes me and he wants more than just a stolen kiss, but I've put the brakes on it. Right now, I don't know how much longer I can stall him or hide my feelings."

Again, she doesn't respond right away. Obviously, she's carefully thinking about what she wants to say.

"My husband noticed Logan's feelings for you and we have talked about it. So many of the men have found love here that it's hard to ignore, but it's also a very hard line to walk. Recently, I did some research on the history of the Oakside plantation. It turns out that one of the women that used to live here was known as a very successful matchmaker. She died here on the property. All the time that I lived here by myself in this huge house, I never felt the spirits or ghosts or anything like that, but I was never terribly lonely either."

"Maybe she's here wanting to match make all these guys," I tease.

"You joke, but that's a very good possibility. You and Logan are both adults and I'm sure you can manage a relationship very well. But not within the walls of Oakside. No flaunting it and no open relationships you will keep it professional. If at any point it affects his care, we will then have to remove you and find someone else. His care is what will always remain important to us, but we want him happy too. Noah says that he's been extremely happy with you and the thought of you. We won't stand in the way of that. Noah will have a talk with him as well to lay down the rules, but I really appreciate you coming to me and talking to me about it," she says. Then she leans in and gives me a hug.

That was easier than I thought. Though I don't think my conversation with Logan will be quite as easy.

•••••••••••

Logan

Seeing Faith out there holding that little baby and smiling at him like he was the center of her world made me realize I can never give her that. I also realized she would be an amazing mom if given the chance, and I can't rob her of it.

How could I be a father? I can't talk to my kids. I'd never be able to get their attention, be able to stop them from danger, or even tell them why they can't do this or that. Parenting would solely rest on the mom, and that isn't fair either.

Growing up, all I wanted was to find the love my grandparents had. It wasn't perfect. They fought, and they didn't always agree, but they had love, respect, and kindness. They might be mad as all get out at each other, but my grandma was the first to stand up for my grandpa and vice versa.

Though I may not have been interested in anything too serious while I was deploying and constantly moving around, I did still want to fall in love, get married and have kids. I wanted to grow old with someone, to sit on the front porch and watch grandkids playing in the yard.

She asked me to write down how I was feeling and I'm not sure if it's her that wants to know or my ASL teacher. Suddenly, I see how messy this can all get if I can't separate the two. Maybe she was on to something when she suggested we take this slowly. It's so easy with her that I forgot I'm not the same person I used to be.

Faith,

Seeing you with that little boy today made me realize how great of a mother you will be someday. Then it hit me that it couldn't be with me. How can I be a parent and not be able to talk to my kids?

How can I keep them safe if I can't yell out when they are in a dangerous situation? I can't take the opportunity to be a mother away from you, either. You are going to be an amazing mom and your kids will be so lucky to have you. I can't deprive your future kids of that.

You were right to say we need to take things slow. My old self, I wouldn't have thought twice about being with you because what I feel is very real and something I haven't felt before.

But now I'm damaged goods and a beautiful and kind girl like you deserves so much more than me.

Logan

Signing my name to what reads like a breakup letter almost shatters my heart. There is a soft knock on the door, and I look up to find Faith there and she looks worried. Still as pretty as ever and she's so beautiful my heart hurts.

You asked me to write my thoughts down, I say.

Handing her the journal, she takes it from me, studying me for a moment before she walks over to the couch and sits. Giving her space, I sit on the opposite side while she reads what I wrote.

"Logan, you really believe all this?" she asks, worry laced in her voice.

I nod because I truly do. In our journal, I am always honest and raw with her. It's the only place I am not constricted with my communication, just by how long my hand can stand to hold the pen.

Every word of it, I say.

Faith gets up and sits down next to me, placing a hand on my arm.

"I understand all those thoughts. You are trying to picture your future and how you and everyone else fit into it. It's what we have always done since we were kids. But you are just dipping your feet in this new reality and trying to swallow the whole whale at once instead of taking it piece by piece.

Your kids will grow up with sign language and won't know any difference. As far as getting their attention, you can still whistle. They will learn ASL from a young age and will probably sign before they are talking.

You not being able to talk will not prevent you from doing anything, but only if you don't let it. There is always a way and I'm here to give you the tools to be able to do it.

You have to stop putting these walls up because in the long run, the only person you are hurting is yourself."

Something about what she says hits me hard. My eyes start to sting, and my throat burns as a wave of emotions runs over me.

"Logan..." her voice is soft as she pulls me in for a hug. I bury my face in her neck and that's when I realize I'm crying.

I couldn't tell you the last time I cried or why. Logan cried during their first meetin Holding on to her for dear life, I cry because I can't stop the emotions. As she was talking, I could picture a whole life of being able to have a family, to be a good father and all of it with her. I can see it so clearly.

Opening to the possibility of it, I released all the emotion I've been trying to keep at bay and now I don't know how to rein it back in.

Chapter 11

Faith

I can't believe we fell asleep on the couch. After checking the time, not more than two hours have gone by. But it's been a very long few days and that little cat nap felt like a full night's sleep.

Logan is still asleep, and this couch is so deep he is on his side, so I'm able to sneak out from under his arm without waking him. It's been a long day for him too. He needs the sleep and I really should be heading home especially, after Lexi's speech earlier today.

Going to his desk, I grab a piece of paper and leave him a note, swapping out the journals. As I pick it up, the journal slips from my hand. Thankfully, it doesn't wake Logan, but it does fall open to one of his recent entries that I have yet to read. A few words on the page get my attention, so I sit down to read it.

Faith,

I know you want to take things slowly, and I understand why. Though I will respect your wishes, know that slow with you is the last thing I want. I feel such a deep connection with you, and I don't know if it's the letters in the journal or simply we've bonded over this time in my life.

Every day, I look forward to seeing you. I can't wait to read what you write me, and then to texting with you at night. There is definitely a deep level of connection and it's not something I've ever experienced.

I want you to know I'm not going anywhere. When my treatment is done, I will go slow and be here waiting for my chance. Already I'm anticipating and excited to take you out on our first date.

The thought is scary as hell, but only because it means so much. I don't want to mess things up. But even more, it would be my first big outing since losing my voice, which also worries me a bit too.

Though being scared means I'm outside my comfort zone and that I'm growing as a person. At least that's what they tell me here, anyway.

Even though I know I'm rambling, I wanted to tell you I think I'm falling for you, and that doesn't scare me one bit.

Logan

By the time I'm done reading the entry, I have tears in my eyes and movement beside me catches my attention.

You weren't supposed to read that until you got home, Logan signs.

His hair is slightly messy, and he has that just woke up look. Since I don't know what to say, I don't say anything. Instead, I get up and walked past him to the door. Closing it, I lock it. Not really thinking other than I really feel the same as he does, and I want to show him.

Then I walk over to him and right into his arms. He catches me a second before I kiss him. Though he's stunned for a moment, his hands move up to frame my face and take control of the most passionate kiss I've ever had in my life.

Guiding me over to the couch, I fall into his lap all while we're still kissing. I straddle his lap, taking control of the kiss while his hands slide down to cup my breasts. His hand on me, even over my clothes feels so damn good.

Then his hands move down to my hips, pulling me closer so my core is right over his hard erection. Even the slight amount of pressure feels incredible. So good, I can't stop moaning. He smiles, but brings his hands up.

You have to be quiet, sweetheart.

I nod because I know I do. His hands make their way back to my waist and slowly peel off my shirt. My hair falls to the side when I lean down to kiss him. Her hands move all over my exposed skin and the sensations races across my body and down to my core.

I want to see his body too, so I reach for his shirt and he freezes, and I stop.

What's wrong? I ask.

For a moment, he doesn't meet my eyes. When he looks at me, there's worry there.

I have scars from the crash. They aren't pretty.

But they are a part of you, and I want all of you, not just the pretty parts. I tell him, but also seeing the doubt on his face. When I reach for his shirt again, he doesn't move.

I slowly peel his shirt off, giving him plenty of time to stop me if he wants to, but he doesn't. His shirt joins mine on the floor as I get the first look at his scars.

He sits perfectly still as I look them over. I've already seen glimpses of the one around his neck, but never thought much of it. That scar travels down over his shoulder and chest. There are cuts and what look like some burn marks. The skin is raised and pink, but all healed.

Slowly, I trace the scars starting at his neck, moving down over his shoulder, and then over his chest.

"To you, these scars remind you of a day I'm sure you'd rather forget," I whisper. "But to me, they are a symbol that you survived, and that you were stronger than that crash."

Very gently and slowly, I kiss each scar. I take my time even when he throws his head back on the couch and his breathing increases. When I'm done, tears are flowing down his face, but he doesn't give me time to even speak as he pulls me in for another kiss and lays me down on the couch, arms braced over me.

Takings his time kissing my exposed skin, he removes my bra, causing my nipples to pebble. With agonizing slowness, he kisses my breasts, sucking on my nipples, driving me crazy before he stands and strips us both until we're naked.

"Condom?" I ask, praying he has one because I don't want to stop.

I got us covered. He smiles and reaches into the coffee table drawer and pulls one out.

Later, I'm going to ask him about it, but not right now. I just want him inside of me. Right now, this minute. Reaching out for his hand when he is done rolling the condom on, I pull him to me. When he lays over me, caging me in, I love the feeling of being protected by him.

His big muscles around me make me feel safe and sheltered. As the tip of his cock nudges me, I spread my legs and wrap them around his hips. Then he slides into me.

Being so full of him, is one that holds more emotion than I was expecting. The slow slide of his cock thrusting in and out of me feels amazing, like nothing I could have expected.

He goes slowly, like we have all the time in the world. When all I want to do is cum, he changes things up, drawing out my pleasure. His hands travel all over my body until they finally begin playing with my clit. Then he changes the angle of his thrusts.

The tingles I was feeling before are magnified as I cum, needing to bite his shoulder to keep quiet. When his whole body stiffens, I know he's found his release too. Knowing it's because of me is overwhelming.

Now more than ever, there is no walking away from this man.

Even if it costs me my job.

Chapter 12

Logan

I have a rare day with no doctor appointments during the week. Faith will still be in later before dinner so that leave most of my day free. Though I'm not sure what to do with myself.

Normally, my days are packed with appointments and activities. But they schedule in rest days like today and I have been looking forward to the downtime. I'm thinking of taking a look at what is on TV when Noah peeks his head in.

"Hey, they are starting construction on the new aquatics center. Want to take a walk with me and check it out? We can get some signing practice in on the way," he says.

I nod and look at the tablet, thinking about bringing it just in case.

"Leave it. Let's see if we can both do without talking," he challenges.

So, I leave the tablet, my only way of speaking to people who don't sign and head out with him. Faith and I have been doing really well in what she calls silent conversations and I think as long as the other person can sign, I can get along well. It's when I run into people who can't sign that I find the problems.

But I will have Noah at my side if anything should happen, so I feel comfortable leaving the tablet, especially here at Oakside. I try not to think about when I am no longer here. Those thoughts have been creeping in more and more lately.

I follow Noah out the back of the lobby to the backyard of Oakside.

We have gotten funding much faster than we ever expected. We recently had a large donation from the band Highway 55. So now that the barn is done and underway, we moved on to the aquatic center, Noah signs.

What will the aquatics center include? I ask.

There will be a large swimming pool for therapy use. Hot tub, sauna, steam therapy. Also, we'll have one of those resistance pools and there will also be a heated outdoor pool for residents to use for fun with a doctor's approval.

It sounds like it's going to be a great addition to Oakside, and an expensive one at that. There aren't any places I know of like Oakside, but from what Faith has told me there is one out in Texas. Oakside is gaining popularity thanks to the PR they are getting in the area.

How long will it take to build? I ask.

The outdoor pool will be ready to go in about six months. The aquatic building, they quoted a year, but we are planning for longer than that. My father-in-law is overseeing it and it's the biggest project he's ever worked on, so he's thinking it will take longer than that. It will move faster once the building is up and the roof is on. Before that, we are at the mercy of the weather.

Makes sense, I say.

I may not be from around here, but even I know the south Georgia weather can give you days of great weather only to take it away in a flash and rain for days straight, too.

We walk back beyond the tree line that borders a large backyard. It used to be the house that Oakside was before it was turned into the rehabilitation home it is now.

We decided to keep the tree line to block the building. That way we can keep the yard and sense of being at home. The building isn't going to win any beauty contests so we don't want our patients to be forced to stare at it, he signs.

I'm sure it will be cheaper to not have to worry about the looks of it.

Oh, for sure, Noah says.

Another patient walks up to us. Then he signs, *Hello, I'm Corey.*

I stand there in shock while Noah has a huge smile on his face.

My sister was born deaf, so my family knows ASL, Corey signs as if answering my unspoken question.

I'm Logan. I can hear, but can no longer speak. I point to the scar on my neck and he nods in understanding.

We are heading to the aquatic center to check out the progress and I've challenged myself to not speak the whole time. Care to join us? Noah asks though his signs are a bit slow like he's trying to remember each one.

Happy to, Corey says.

We follow Noah through the new path in the trees coming out the other end. There is a large area of land all cleared and leveled already. It looks much bigger then I imagined it would be.

This week they will be digging the area for the pools and next week pouring the foundation. We have a temporary road built that goes by our house to keep construction noise to a minimum at Oakside. Lexi is just thrilled, Noah says, rolling his eyes.

Both Corey and I smile at that. We walk with Noah for a while and he gets tripped up on a few construction words while signing, but Corey is right there to help him out. So we both learn more together.

Noah tells us how all this land, as well as his and Lexi's home next door, used to be part of the original plantation. Although, their house is newer.

Want to have lunch with me? Corey asks as we head back toward the main building.

I nod, and we go in to get out food, getting a table by the window.

What branch of the service? Corey asks the standard questions that get asked around here.

Navy. I was a pilot and was in a plane crash. You? I ask.

Marine. Was shot in the leg and then when they were trying to get me back to camp a nearby building exploded and the bullet in my leg shifted, causing problems with my ACL and all. I've been here a few months. I'm walking, but not where I need to be to return to active duty. There is talk about discharging me. He shrugs like it doesn't bother him, but I haven't met a person here yet that getting discharged doesn't bother.

Well, I hope you are able to go back. I try to be positive.

Honestly, I don't, he smiles.

I sit there in shock. *Why not?*

I only joined to pay for college. If they medically discharge me, then I can focus full time on college, and they will pay for it.

What do you want to major in at college? I ask.

I want to be a physical therapist. Now more than ever, seeing how much mine helped me. I think I will be in a better position to help. Especially, if I can get a job at a place like Oakside, he says.

I think you will, too. Though I wish I had a plan in place. Without figuring out something, I can see how my life outside this place is going to go. Now that everything has changed, along with my life.

It doesn't have to. My sister works in a graphic design job where she deals solely with emails. Her company has given her a translator to communicate with people who prefer to deal on the phone or in person, he tells me, pausing to drink some of his sweet tea.

She is married to a guy who can hear. In order to ask her out, he learned sign language. They are married now with three kids. He does some translating for her, but she is able to communicate a lot on her own with the help of translation software on her phone.

I hadn't really thought about what I wanted to do job wise, but knowing how accommodating an employer can be gives me hope of finding a good one.

There isn't anything she can't do. Though she just has to do it in a modified way. My parents didn't treat her differently than me and my brother. They expected the same things from her. But they just made the necessary accommodations. She went to a school for the deaf and at home they made sure one of us was around to translate for needed things like doctor appointments and such.

When she was thirteen, we found a doctor who signs, and it's becoming more and more common that doctors will sign to communicate. It's all about who you surround yourself with, he says.

Words I have heard from Faith before. To be careful who I surround myself with and to start meeting people in the deaf community to make connections.

Will people like your sister who are truly deaf even want to help me when I can hear but not talk? I ask the one question I haven't been able to ask Faith.

There is no difference between them. They might ask for your help here and there, but if you can't speak, then you are no different from them in their eyes. The community will welcome you. You get a few people who might get vocal, but you will find they are outsiders thinking they know how people like my sister think.

I really appreciate you answering my questions, I tell him.

Well, I appreciate the chance to sign with you. It's been a while and I want to practice more, so I'm not rusty when I see my sister again in a few months. If you are up for it, I'd like to have lunch with you every day. I can help answer questions, you can help me practice, and we can both use the company.

I know Faith will be ecstatic about me making a new friend especially someone with connections to ASL and the deaf community. Part of me wonders if Noah's motivation for a walk centered around this to begin with.

I'd like that. I need practice as well. My girl has been pushing me to find other people who sign and to meet other people here. I can't stop the big smile that covers my face as I refer to Faith as my girl for the first time.

After talking with Corey today, I finally see a glimmer of a future. It's a small hope, but it's there and I can't wait to build on it.

Hopefully, Faith is willing to come along for the ride.

Chapter 13

Faith

This week, I'm going to dinner with my brother and his wife at their house. My parents will be there too and it's the first time we have all been able to get together since both my brother and parents were traveling.

None of them know how serious things have gotten with me and Logan, and I'm not sure what to do. So on the way, I call my best friend Lauren, who recently was in the same situation at Oakside with her soon to be husband.

"Hey girl, what are you up to tonight?" she asks, picking up the phone.

"On the way to dinner with my parents and my brother."

"Then why do you sound so nervous?" Concern laces her voice.

"Things have gotten serious with Logan and I haven't told them. The last time anything was mentioned was with my brother, and he was pretty concerned with Logan being my patient and all."

"How serious are things? The last I heard, you were taking it slow while you were still working with him," she says. The background noise quiets as the sound of a door closing indicated she probably moved to her bedroom away from her family.

"Well, he admitted he's falling for me, and hasn't been shy about telling me how serious he is and how he feels. Oh, and we slept together," I admit.

It's been nice to have a guy who is up front with his feelings. There is no guessing and no wondering what he means when he says this or that. I know how he feels about me, and there's no doubt.

"Wow. How do you feel about him?" She asks the million dollar question.

"I really like him. I haven't felt anything like this and I want to get to know him. If it was out of Oakside, I wouldn't even be questioning it. But being he's still my patient, so I'm hesitant. Even though I told Lexi, it still has me worried if it were to get out. We both know it's not exactly looked upon lightly in our professional world."

"But how do you feel about him? I don't care about the excuses, the reasons, or what you should or shouldn't do. Forget everyone's approval, or if it gets out. How does this man make you feel?" she asks.

When I really think about it, a big smile covers my face. Then I pull over to the side of the road in front of an empty lot before I turn on to my brother's street.

"Logan makes me happy. The thought of going to see him gives me butterflies, and I crave his touch. I feel safe in his arms and if I'm honest, I think I'm falling for him, too." I whisper the last part.

"That's what I thought. So I have two words for you. Fuck it," she says in all seriousness.

"Lauren!" I gasp, not expecting that from her, of all people.

"Well, if I had listened, then Gavin and I wouldn't be together. Brooke wouldn't have her husband Luke, and Mandy and Levi wouldn't have gotten together. You can't always play by the rules when your heart is involved.

You can find another job, and Lexi would be happy to bring you back if you were honest with her. But you won't find love again. If you think that is where this is going, then don't let it pass you by because you are scared. You don't have to tell your family anything. Not now, not if you don't want to."

"I don't know how much choice I will have. I know my brother will ask and that will prompt my mom and dad to start asking questions. It will be worse if I try to avoid it."

"So, give them a generic we are taking it slow and seeing where it is going answer," she says and I can picture her shrugging because she is a very easy going, it's just that simple kind of person.

"Guess we will see. I'm right down the road, so I'll let you go and text you tonight." I sigh, wishing I had a reason to stay on the phone all night.

"Alright girl, I'll be sending good vibes your way and I can't wait to meet Logan officially!"

Taking a moment more to collect my thoughts, I calm my nerves before getting back on the road and to my brother's. After getting myself under control, I pull into his driveway. Whatever happens, I don't need to give anyone a reason to pry into my life.

By the time I get up to the porch to knock on the front door, I feel much calmer and more relaxed.

Dawn answers, pulling me in to a warm hug.

"Tonight, we are telling your parents that I'm pregnant. They don't know yet," she whispers into my ear.

Well at least that will give everyone something to focus on that isn't me. So I squeeze her a little harder as a silent thank you, even though she has no idea for what.

I go into the living room that is to my left, with Dawn right behind me. As soon as I walk in, Mom jumped up and hugged me.

"Oh, my baby, we missed you!" She says, squeezing me way too tight.

"Mom, you weren't gone that long," I tell her, trying to pull out of the hug.

"It felt much longer with all the boring things your father had planned. Lord, I'd have rather watched paint dry," she huffs.

"Dear, you were told I had to work, and you were more than welcome to stay home. I told you it wasn't going to be a fun little vacation." He pulls her to his side in a hug, I'm pretty sure was more to silence her than anything else.

"Faith, come sit with me and let's catch up," my brother says, rescuing me.

"Mom, why don't you go help Dawn? She has been wanting to learn your gravy recipe." At my brother's words, Mom runs off to the kitchen.

"I noticed your rain gutter extension came off. I'm going to go fix it before dinner." Dad says, going outside leaving just my brother and me.

"When you got home from your business trip, did she greet you like she hadn't seen you in decades too?" I ask.

"Oh yes, and the guilt for not calling her every day of the trip," he chuckles. "Now tell me about the guy."

I smile, looking down at my hands in my lap.

"We are going slow and getting to know each other. But he has made it clear he plans to take me out to dinner once he is out of Oakside."

"I'm glad you two are taking your time. Though I worry he has a fixation on you because you are helping him heal and I don't want you to get hurt once he's out of there and his attention wanes."

Shaking my head, I say, "Logan isn't like that. He's committed to learning, but he's scared too. The writing of the journals back and forth has allowed us both to open up in a way I really hadn't planned when I suggested writing to each other."

"Life is what happens when you are busy making other plans," he recited the quote we heard all the time growing up.

"So, when do you plan to tell them?" I whisper.

"Tonight, at dessert. Dawn has something special planned."

"Dinner is ready. Oh, where on Earth did your father go?" Mom says, stepping into the living room.

"I'm right here, dear. I just went out to fix something I had noticed when we got here," Dad says.

"Well, go wash up it's time to eat."

We all pile into my brother's dining room and the one empty chair beside me doesn't go unnoticed. It's a big reminder that I don't have someone and that if things were different Logan could be the one sitting there.

Maybe next time we have family dinner here, he will be. The thought of bringing Logan home to meet my family doesn't fill me with dread and make me sick like it did the last guy I dated. Instead, I can't wait to bring him home and for my family to meet him and for him to meet them.

Dinner went smoothly, and we talked about my parents' trip and then my brother's recent trip. All the traveling talk has me starting to feel like maybe it's time for me to plan a vacation.

"When will you be taking a vacation, dear?" Mom asks, reading my mind.

"Oh, I don't know. The thought of traveling alone doesn't appeal to me much." I shake my head.

"Well, you won't be alone for long. What about the guy you told us about last time?" Dawn asks.

I glare at her, and I can tell my brother kicks her under the table.

"You are seeing someone? Tell us all about him! What does he do? Do we know his parents? How serious is it?" My mom fires off questions and Dawn looks apologetic, but I will make her pay for this.

"It's nothing Mom. I'm just talking to someone. We are taking it slow."

"You seemed pretty serious last time." Dawn says, proving she isn't sorry.

"Dawn, seriously?" I snap.

She opens her mouth to say something, but my brother stops her.

"Well, we should meet him." My dad says, and I know it's not negotiable.

"I will talk to him and see. Not sure if we are to that point." I tell them to prepare them in case Oakside doesn't allow him off the property or if Logan just isn't ready for an outing yet.

"Well dear, make it happen. We have been so worried about you and not dating." Mom turns the guilt on.

"Is it time for dessert yet? I heard Dawn has a surprise for you." I put the attention back to her and her eyes go wide.

"Oh, um yes. Why don't you all go sit in the living room and I will bring it out," Dawn says, jumping up.

"I need to use the restroom." I head down to the hall and lock myself in the small guest bath and pull out my phone.

Me: My parents want to meet you because I made the mistake of telling my brother about you and his wife can't keep a secret.

Logan: I don't know how I feel about you wanting to keep me your dirty little secret.

Me: it's not that. I just figure my parents' house is the last place you want your first outing to be.

Logan: I think it's a great controlled environment and will let me get to know you better. Let's do it.

Me: Ok, remember I warned you.

Going back to the living room, I sit on the opposite side of the room from my parents.

"Logan said he'd be happy to meet you, but his schedule will be a bit tricky. Actually, he's a patient at Oakside." I rip the Band-Aid off.

"Your patient?" Dad asks.

Nodding, I look down at my hands. I wait for the speech I'm sure I will get about how unprofessional it is, how wrong it is.

"What is he in for?" Dad asks to take control of the conversation.

"He was a Navy pilot and his plane crashed. His voice box was injured. He can hear, but not speak."

"And you have been working with him?"

"Yes, I'm one of the people on his team."

"What are his plans once he leaves Oakside?" Dad asks.

"He's still working on that. It's been a huge adjustment relearning how to communicate, but he's working hard, and they just started him with a career counselor to make plans."

"Well, we look forward to meeting him." Dad says as Dawn walks out.

"We have a gift from our trip for both of you. You have to open them at the same time," Dawn says, handing them each a box.

My brother is recording, and I notice Dawn has changed her clothes and is wearing a button-down shirt she is keeping closed.

"Okay go!" She tells my parents once they are both settled. They open their gifts and it takes them a moment of confusion before the reaction hits them.

My mom burst into full on hysterics and jumps up to hug them both, saying things I can't understand through her emotions.

Getting up, I go look at what was inside my mom's box. She loves baking, so there is a baby size apron, a small toy size rolling pin, and a whisk with a onesie that says 'new baking buddy coming this fall' on it.

I have to give them credit for the super cute idea.

Dad stands up to give a round of hugs and I check out his. During his semi-retirement phase, Dad took up fishing. He still goes a few times a month. So his gift has an engraved fishing lure that says 'New fishing buddy coming this fall.'

It really is a fun way of announcing the baby. As my brother serves up some celebratory cupcakes, my mom and Dawn start talking about all things baby.

Thankfully, the baby takes front and center and no more talk of Logan happens the rest of the night. But I know they won't let me off the hook that easily.

Chapter 14

Logan

As soon as I agreed to dinner, Faith's mom was relentless. She called almost every day when she knew Faith would be with me to get me to agree to a time. I wish it was as simple as checking my calendar and setting a date, but nothing is that easy.

Faith had to get approval from not just my doctors, but Lexi and Noah, too. Of course Lexi was insistent on taking Faith to lunch and having a girl's talk date while Noah talked to me.

He wanted to make sure I knew what I was doing and make sure I was ready for this step. When I assured him I was, he finally agreed to it. Next was to 'set terms with her parents,' as she likes to say.

She insisted dinner to be at her house and for it to be early so I could get back to Oakside at a decent time. Her parents and her brother agreed, and that leads me to now.

Since I got here, I'm getting ready for my first trip out of Oakside. I don't know who is more nervous, me or

Faith. Noah is also here checking in to help calm Faith down.

"You both have my number if you need anything, or anything happens, okay? Don't hesitate to call no matter the time. I kind of wish I had someone to SOS me out of a few dinner meetings with some of my ex's family. They kept me there for hours talking about the craziest stuff," Noah says, shaking his head.

"I hate to say I feel like that is what my parents have planned. Knowing my mom, when she wouldn't agree to lunch, that said it all," Faith says, making my nerves skyrocket.

"You will do fine. I just haven't told them much about you, so they want to learn anything and everything. They are protective and while my mom isn't harping on the whole getting married thing right now because Dawn is pregnant, she was always asking about it before. I think she just won't relax until I'm married off and happy."

"Parents always want wants best for their kids. I'm starting to learn that myself." Noah says referring to his son.

"Alright, let's get going. I still have to cook and all. Before they get there, I want you to get comfortable with my place," Faith says.

Taking my hand, we walk out to the lobby. She stops at the front desk, and I sign out for the evening. Then I follow her out the front door and across to the side of the large plantation home where her car is parked.

When I follow her to her side of the car and open the door for her, she stops and looks at me for a moment.

This is our first date out of Oakside. I plan to do it right, I say.

She smiles, but gets in the car. Leaning in, I give her a quick kiss before closing the door and get in on the passenger side. Though I try to hide how uneasy it makes me because I believe she should be the one relaxing and I drive her anywhere she needs or wants to go.

Leaving the protection of Oakside, my nerves kick it into the next gear and Faith picks up on it instantly.

"Hey, we got this. If it's too much, you just say the word. I have a super comfy reading nook in my bedroom. At any point, you can hang in there to get some space, okay?"

Since she is driving, I pull out the tablet to talk with her. I want her eyes on the road.

"Thank you. Oakside had been a comfort and I normally only deal with one person at a time. Now there will be four focused on me. Five, if I include you."

"Then we need a code word you can do in sign to let me know it's too much. How about blueberry?" she asks. Then since we're at a stoplight, she shows me the sign for blueberry.

It's perfect. Just subtle enough that I don't think it will cause too much attention. Faith reaches over and takes my hand in hers and the connection is comforting. It reminds me I'm not alone.

At the end of a road, we pulled up to a beautiful cottage shaded by oak trees.

"Well, this is home," she says.

I follow her up to the front door.

"Would you like the grand tour?" She asks as we step through the door.

Yes please. I say, taking in the living room.

The room is painted a light gray and there are hardwood floors, but the real color comes from the pops of color around the room in the paintings, throw pillows, rug, and other items you can tell she has handpicked because they all go well together.

"This is the living room and through here is the kitchen and dining room. The back door leads to the back porch, where I can watch some of the best sunsets."

I follow her through the doorway where there is a rather large kitchen and dining area.

"This room is normally the family room where I will relax and watch TV, but it's been taken over by all things wedding planning for Lauren, so it's the wedding cave."

The family room has mostly boxes in it and there are magazines spread around.

Is she having everything shipped to your house? I ask, smiling.

Pretty much. They don't have room at her place, and on top of wedding planning, they are looking to sell their place and buy a new one, so it's easier to have everything sent here.

She goes on to show me two more bedrooms and a guest bath before taking me to her bedroom.

This is why I bought the place. The reading nook sold me, but the bathroom has a clawfoot tub that is perfect for reading and a hot bath.

And now all night all I'm going to picture is you naked in that bathtub, I say.

If you play your cards right, you might get to see that.

I can't wait. I tell her, pulling her into my arms.

My lips barely touch hers when the doorbell rings.

"Dammit, they are here early," she sighs. "Well, what an excuse to get them out of here early. Before I have to take you back, I want some time alone with you."

Perfect because I want some time with you too, I sign. Then place a kiss on her forehead before she goes to answer the door.

"Faith!" A man greets her, pulling her into a bear hug. It set me on edge seeing another man's hands on her.

"Eddy stop. Logan, this is my big brother and his wife Dawn. She just announced the other day she is pregnant," Faith says. Then she hugs the woman walking in the door.

"Guys, this is Logan."

Nice to meet you, Logan, Eddy signs.

Faith looks shocked.

Faith didn't mention you knew how to sign.

"I only learned a few phrases so I'm not sure what you said," Eddy admits.

I appreciate the effort, I say and Faith translates for me.

"Okay, so we wanted to get here early and help cook because this meeting is mostly my fault," Dawn says. "I have my lasagna and garlic bread ready to warm up. If we pop it now, it will be ready just after your parents get here and we can have an early dinner. Blame it on me starving and maybe end the night early."

"That okay?" Faith asks, looking at me and I just nod.

"Come on and help me cook." Dawn grabs Faith's hand and pulls her to the kitchen leaving Eddy and me in the living room.

"Shoot, their goes our translator," Eddy says, sitting on the couch.

Grabbing the tablet, I show him how Faith taught me to use it. We talked about a few things, but mostly about Faith and how she grew up.

Before I know it, her parents are here and join right in on the conversation. Things are going well, and they are patient, waiting for me to reply to questions using the tablet.

Though I should have known it wouldn't last. The moment we sit down for dinner, the questions start.

"So, Logan, what are your plans for after school?" Faith's dad asks.

"Go ahead, I'll translate," Faith says softly next to me.

I met with my career counselor recently at Oakside, and we are exploring my options. The first step is to go back to school. I have my associate's degree but whatever I decide to do I'd like to get my bachelors. The only thing I know for sure is I want to work with other veterans who were injured in action and their families.

Faith translates as I sign, and then we wait for her dad's response.

"I like that they offer a counselor to help you figure out your next phase. What are your next steps with my daughter?"

"Dad! Don't do this," Faith says.

I place my hand on her arm.

It's okay. Tell him my next steps are to date you and get to know you better outside the walls of Oakside.

"What did he say?" her dad asks.

"This is so embarrassing. He says was wants to date me and get to know me better outside of Oakside."

"It will be such a great story to tell the grandkids someday."

"Mom! You already have one grandkid on the way. Be happy with that and let me be!" Faith buries her head in her hands.

"One isn't enough!" her mom says.

I laugh because she reminds me of one of those old sitcom moms.

"Mom! Way to make us not feel important!" Her brother says, but you can tell he really isn't offended he's just trying to take the attention away from his sister.

"There is plenty of love to go around. Don't you worry, dear," her mom says.

"Okay, let's try to make Logan feel welcome and not want to run for the hills, okay?" Faith says.

That seems to catch her mom's attention as she looks over at me.

The rest of the night is calm, and they are more respectful. They are also gone before six p.m. thanks to the early dinner. This gives me some time alone with Faith.

"All I want is to lie down and cuddle with you. I will set an alarm in case we doze off, but I'm not going to fight to stay awake," she says.

Let's do it.

There is nothing I want more than her in my arms.

Chapter 15

Faith

Waking up, I find myself snuggling with Logan on my couch. It takes me a few minutes to reorient myself. After my parents and my brother left, we started cuddling and I guess we both drifted off. Checking the time, it's just after eight and I know Noah isn't expecting us back until around ten or so.

Even though it's tempting to curl back up and go back to sleep with him, we have some completely alone time and I don't want to waste it. So, I took a moment to enjoy watching him sleeping on my couch. Thankfully, I went for an oversized couch, but his large body makes it look normal sized and fits us both.

He's lying on his back with one arm up behind his head and the other wrapped around me. Very slowly, I slide down his body and out of his arms. When we decided to snuggle on the couch, he slipped out of his jeans so he's just in his boxers and t-shirt.

He's semi hard, so I run my hand over his length and watch to make sure I'm not waking him up. He doesn't stir, but he does get hard, so I gently rub him and once he's fully hard, I pull him from his boxers and run my tongue over the tip of his cock.

That is what finally causes him to wake, so I waste no time taking him in my mouth. I enjoying the way his body tenses as he grips his hair before his eyes pop open and land on me. For a moment, in what also looks like a brief prayer, he closes his eyes. Then both of his hands run through my hair encouraging me to take more of him.

For a brief moment, I wonder what it would be like to him groan in pleasure. What dirty words would he say while I'm going down on him? Not having those sounds forced me to pay attention to the cues his body is giving me.

I can tell he's fighting his orgasm because every muscle in his body is tense and his breathing is rapid. So when he tries to pull me off of him, I double down, taking him all the way to the back of my throat and swallowing around him.

He explodes in my mouth, and I suck down every drop. Not stopping, I continue teasing the tip with my tongue, running it over the ridge of the head of his cock and watching the little aftershocks that overtake him.

That is one hell of a way to wake up, he signs.

"There are advantages of having alone time, so I'd thought I'd show you one." I say as I climb back up his body to snuggle back into him.

Right before I lay down, he flips me over and cages me in. Wrapping my arms around his, we stare at each other for a moment before he rests his forehead on mine and closes his eyes. I close mine too and we soak in being this close to each other, with no one interrupting us.

Making it clear it's my turn, he kisses my neck and down to my belly, and then slowly lowers my pants. Only he doesn’t pull my pants all the way down, which limits my movement. Then he spreads me as wide as he can, not bothering to remove my panties, and pulls them to the side.

He circles my clit with his tongue and my body tenses up and I couldn't stop the moan if I tried. He doubles down, driving me crazy, and all I can do is hold on to the couch for dear life. To say Logan is talented with his tongue is an understatement. Just as I’m ready to fall over the edge, he stopped.

Then he kisses the sides of my thighs.

"Logan!" I gasp, gripping his head.

Giving me an evil smile, he continues kissing my thighs before he moves back to my clit. In no time at all, I can feel every one of the strokes of his tongue as if it's all over my body. When he sucks on my clit again, I orgasm so hard that my pussy spasms and my back arches, trying to get closer to him.

When he relents and I finally start to relax, he crawls back up my body, pulling me into him and putting the blanket over us as we snuggle.

There is no talking. We just hold each other until my alarm goes off. Even though we get dressed, neither of us moves off the couch just yet.

I think I want to go to a school for graphic design. It was a hobby while I was in the military and didn't have to take calls, he says.

I realize I have yet to teach him of the call service he can use. So I explain. "There is a service where you can basically use a Tele-Interpreter and make phone calls. They go through a third party who will have you on video and can translate what you say and since you can hear what they say, that person will basically be your voice as needed," I tell him, pulling up the service for him.

"The service is more common than you think and there are a few companies that offer it now."

This is great. Thank you, he says. Then he takes a look at it on his tablet. *Oh, I met another one of the guys the other day. His name is Corey, and his sister was born deaf. He saw me signing with Noah and introduced himself. We had lunch together and are meeting up again later this week so he can keep up on his sign language for when he goes to see his sister again.*

"Logan, that is great!" I tell him, hugging him. I'm so excited for him. "When people who know you see you using ASL, I think they'll want to learn or practice what they know. Like my family, for instance. Even though I've been teaching it for years, you are really the first person they have interacted with that they needed to know sign language. What makes me really happy is they took the first step and learned a bit just for you."

When he smiles, I can tell the ease and how comfortable this meeting with my family helped to calm some of his nerves. It's the first of many events outside Oakside for him and I think with how smooth this one went, he will enter them more confidently now.

"I hate to take you, but I think it's time I get you back to Oakside," I say, looking at the clock once again.

Thank you for having me here. It's great to see where you live and be able to picture you in this space now, he says.

We get ready to go and he's nothing short of a perfect gentleman opening my car door again before getting into the car on his side.

After dropping him off, I allow my thoughts to wander to the day when he doesn't have to go back to Oakside and we are living together. No more nights apart.

My heart wants that image badly.

• • • • ● ● • ● • • • •

Logan

Hey, where are you heading? Noah asks as we run into each other in the hallway.

Down to have lunch with Corey.

I'll walk with you. I just saw you mentioned doing some graphic design, and I did some research and found a professor in Savannah that teaches several of the courses and is also fluent in ASL. If you plan to stay in the area, I think he will be a good fit for you, he says.

I hadn't given it much thought. With Faith in the picture, I guess I just assumed I'd be staying in the area. This is a talk I need to have with Faith. How does she see us working out when I leave here? Because I feel like that is coming up sooner than we both realize.

After meeting Corey in the lobby, we go in to grab our lunch.

So, tell me about your girl, he says.

Actually, she is the girl here who is teaching me ASL. She is kind and sweet and likes me despite not being able to talk.

So what if you can't talk. You will be a great listener and that's all women want at the end of the day. Anyway, it won't matter to the right woman. Don't settle because you think she is the only one who will like you.

No, I definitely don't feel like I'm settling with her. I'm still in shock she wants anything to do with me. She's smart and cute as hell. While she could have any guy, she wants me. Though I feel like she is settling with me, yet I'm holding on for dear life. So I'm doing everything I can to keep her.

I'm not sure what kind of life I can even offer Faith. Everything changed when I lost my voice. Really, I don't know what a life with me looks like anymore.

Well, I just talked to my sister the other day and told her about you, Corey says. *They invited you to dinner when you are finally released from this joint. I think it would be a good idea for you to see her and how she manages. She works, has kids, a family and nothing holds her back. From the outside looking in, you'd never know she was deaf.*

I'd like that. It would be great to meet someone else who is crushing it in life and can inspire me. Maybe the life I want isn't so far away, I say.

That life is a lot closer than you realize. One thing my parents told my sister over and over growing up was, don't use your lack of hearing as a disability. I'll flip it for you. Don't use your lack of voice as a disability. It's an easy excuse on why you can't do this or that and no one would blame you. But why not amaze them with all the things that you can do despite not having your voice?

We went on to talk more about his sister growing up. How all the struggles that she faced and the different ways she overcame them. After lunch I went back up to my room to wait on Faith.

Once I'm back in my room, all I can think about is what our future could look like. I'm assuming she'd stay between Savannah and here, working teaching sign language like she has been.

Though it would be great to work from home doing graphic design. It's not necessarily something I'd have to be in an office to do. The thought of having kids still scares me, but knowing that she believes in me enough means that I'm not going to stop trying to make it work. Because she's right, I can whistle to get their attention if needed and we'd raise the kids knowing sign language from the start, which will make things a lot easier.

I can see me being a work at home dad taking kids to school or picking them up. I'd work at home during the day. Then I'd have dinner ready to spoil her when she comes home in the evening. Though I always thought that my wife would be the one to stay home with the kids. But then again, I always thought that I would be lifelong military as well. Now I'm liking the idea of working from home, so we don't have to put the kids in daycare and Faith can still continue to do what she loves.

Another thing I'd like to do is volunteer here, helping the men and women as much as possible because this place has given me so much. It's all within my grasp, but I don't want to get too far ahead of myself. The next step will be to see how Faith pictures things with us. How does she picture her future? Because there's nothing I wouldn't do to give her whatever it is she wants.

If she wants to be the stay at home mom, I'd gladly make that happen. We could both work from home. She can be the PTO mom and I can be the sports dad. Once again, I have to remind myself to take a deep breath and not get too far ahead.

First, I have to make plans with Faith.

Chapter 16

Faith

I need to go see Logan, but I'm running behind. Most of the morning, I've been on the phone with the hospital about another patient who has lost their hearing.

He was transferred from the Germany hospital and they're assessing his injuries and looking to send him to Oakside. Apparently, he's got some family that would also need to learn sign language to communicate with him. They live about thirty minutes away and would be able to visit often, but his sister would need to learn virtually because she lives across the country.

His family is anxious to start learning now. As soon as the hospital can clear him, they will be transferring him to Oakside. The hospital is thinking that would happen within the next week or two.

Logan's doing so much better that my time with him is coming to an end soon. While it does bring a bit of sadness, I'm also excited to see what it can do for our relationship as well.

Taking on another patient here at Oakside will keep us close, at least until he leaves.

When I get to his room, I find him on the couch, staring out the window. Seeing me, his face lights up. There's just something wonderful knowing that you can do that to someone and be that person for them.

How has your day been? I ask.

Pretty good. I had lunch with Corey and have been thinking.

I'm hoping he means he's been thinking in a good way, but I'm still not sure.

Oh yeah, thinking about what? I ask.

Mostly about us and what our relationship looks like once I leave here, he says.

What do you see when you're thinking about once you leave here? I ask.

Well, I want to know what you see when you think about us in the future, he says, putting me on the spot.

I have no idea what type of answer he's looking for or how far in the future he's looking. But I guess it's best to just be honest as honest as I possibly can.

I see us building a life together. Want to be there and support you with whatever you decide to do, whether that's graphic design or something else that catches your eye. I like to think that we're moving toward commitment, towards building a family together. I see raising a family with kids who know sign language and have the ability to be bilingual. It would be wonderful to have kids who have the desire to help volunteer at places like this because they understand how much it helps other people like their dad. Then I stop to really think about where I see us five years from now.

Five years down the road, I see us living a normal life where there is nothing that we can't have or do. Our life is good and we're happy. I translate for you as needed and we surround ourselves with people who are willing to accept you for you and either know or learn sign language.

When I added that last bit, something in his mood shifted and I can't pinpoint exactly what or why. He seems like he's off and maybe just going through the motions for the rest of the afternoon.

"Are we okay? You just seem a little off," I ask, wanting to make sure that I didn't say something to upset him and that I have a chance to fix it if I did before I leave for the night.

Yeah, it's just a lot to think about and if I'm being honest, I'm pretty tired.

While it's a legit answer, something in my gut tells me it's also a cop-out as well. But I decide not to push him as he's thinking about the future and that's all that matters right now. We don't have to have our whole lives planned all at once and it's probably better that we don't, so we're not disappointed if things turn out differently.

Things are just not right as we say goodbye. Even though he kisses me goodnight, it's on my mind as I go to my car.

"Faith, do you have a minute?" Noah stops me on my way out to the car.

"Of course, is everything okay?" I ask.

"Oh yes, everything is fine. Let me walk you to your car and we can talk on the way. Basically, I just want to talk to you about how Logan's doing. He seems to be moving forward and doing well. His career counselor said that he's got a solid plan in place they're working towards that so he can go back to school. He seems to have no blocks communicating that, so I wanted to touch base with you."

"I think he has all the tools in place that he needs as far as communicating. I've shown him how to use the tablet and he's picked up sign language pretty well. If he needs to learn something else, he knows where to go. I've got him connected with a phone service that will help him with phone calls, but I think the biggest thing he has to overcome now is his own nerves. If I was able to plan some outings with him to do some normal basic everyday things like going to a restaurant and ordering, I think that it would help. Also, going to the grocery store, going to the mall, that sort of thing so he can learn and have the confidence to overcome those conversation barriers," I tell him.

"I agree. I'm really proud of how many guys around here have picked up sign language to have a basic conversation with him. Moreover, I think that people in his life that really truly want to be there will do the same thing. He just needs to give them the chance. And I agree about getting him outside of Oakside. I think it's just what he needs."

“He's close to being ready to leave,” Noah continues. “And he needs to get a game plan in place of where he's going to go and what he's going to do. Though it's a slightly abnormal situation with you two being together, but I figure that's something that the two of you will need to discuss. So I wanted to give you a heads up that if he has a plan in place and wanted to leave, I would sign off on it. But I wanted to make sure that we're not sending him out before he's ready."

"I agree. He was just having a conversation about where we saw each other in the future. I think it's on his mind. I didn't bring it up to him, but I think I'll talk to him about it tomorrow. One option is for him to move in with me. He'd be close, so he could go to school and I'd still be there to help him if he needs it. I know you had mentioned volunteering here and helping out, so that way he'd still be close as well."

"Sounds good. I will let you talk to him and see where his head is. If you'll let me know as I don't want to upset him by bringing it up if he's not really ready." Noah says, opening my car door for me.

"Sounds like a plan. When I talk to him, I will let you know."

On the way home, the vision I had been thinking of Logan and me a few years down the road played in Technicolor. Now it’s much stronger and seems within reach.

When I get home, I take a look at my house through new eyes. The only person I've ever lived with outside of my parents was Lauren, and she was really easy to live with. She had a son, so she did so much of the cleaning and food cooking because she planned it around him.

But I've gotten accustomed to being on my own and I know that it would be a big difference for a guy to move in with me at this point in my life.

Would I lose the reading nook in my bedroom? I know Logan would need his own space, but I can easily make him an office in one of the spare bedrooms. Or maybe he'd settle with the garage as I rarely use it. So it's really no big deal for me to give up the space because it's mostly storage. If I were to go through the stuff, I bet it would be things that I don't even need.

Giving him a home office and free range of the garage in exchange for me keeping my reading nook seems like a pretty good trade off. We can redecorate the rest of the house together.

With a solid plan in place, I sent a text to Logan just checking again to make sure that he's okay. Then I make myself dinner. The entire time I tried to convince myself that the fact that I didn't hear from him right away doesn't mean anything. Maybe he went to play cards with his friends or maybe he can't hear the phone.

I just know I will have a text in the morning.

Chapter 17

Logan

My phone goes off with Faith's text. It's the same one I get every few days and today it almost breaks me and my resolve that I'm doing the right thing.

Faith: I hope you are safe and I'm still here if you need anything. Anything at all. I miss you.

After my talk with her, I realized that I needed to prove not just to her but to myself that she wouldn't need to always be around to translate. Something in me broke thinking that I'd be dependent on her for any part of my life. Without any doubts, I need to know that I could take care of her and prove it to myself before we could have any kind of life together. But even more so, I want her to know that, too.

So after she left that day, I went and talked to Noah, telling him how I felt and what I wanted to do. Even though he thought I should talk to Faith first, he supported me on what I wanted, so long as I kept in touch to let him know I was okay.

Agreeing, I took the coward's way out instead of talking to Faith. I left her a letter because I know she would have tried to talk me out of it. I know I would've caved and it was hard enough thinking about leaving her anyway.

I was scared to death, but I was able to get a hotel room all on my own and was even able to buy a car. After driving for a day, I stopped to order lunch, which was pretty easy.

Giving up the convenience of the drive through, I walked inside, looked at the menu, decided what I wanted, and wrote it in the notes app on my phone. Then I got in line and when it was my turn, I showed the cashier what I wanted. She was nice, put my order in and that was that. Something that had seemed so scary before was so easy.

Where I stopped to get food was close to a park, so I ate in the fresh air and then walked the path around the park, which led me to seeing 'a now hiring' sign in a stone yard.

I had a speech typed up on my tablet about how I could hear but not talk and why. Told them I was a hard worker and took direction well. They hired me on the spot, and I started the next day.

The guys I work with were pretty leery but once I proved that I did my job and didn't cause problems they accepted me. It was nice to be working again. On my days off, I tried new things like going to the movies, concerts and some stores. All the things I hoped to do with Faith one day, I went out and practiced.

I took myself out to a restaurant, ordered food, and had an entire experience with no problems. Then went to the movies, ordered popcorn and enjoyed my movie with no trouble. I successfully navigated going shopping and all the little things that pop up in life.

I've been messaging with Corey and realized I'm only an hour from his family's place. Maybe subconsciously I planned it that way, so when he invited me over for dinner, it was a no brainer. Plus, I haven't had a home cooked meal in a really long time and it would be great to eat something that isn't microwaved.

As I pull up to the address that he gave me, I find him playing in the front yard with two younger boys. Probably nephews, I'm assuming.

I'm glad you made it. Everyone's looking forward to meeting you. Let's head inside, he says.

We enter the house and for a house full of people, it was pretty quiet. Maybe out of respect for his sister because everyone is using sign language. I have to say, it's a sight to see.

Early on I asked Faith to do a mixture of sign language and talking because I loved hearing her voice. But I can understand when you have someone who doesn't hear, then unless they can read lips, you would sign instead of speak. Though it's still really eerie, to hear nothing but the cooking sounds from the kitchen.

After Corey makes the introductions to his nieces and nephews with a bunch of names that I won't remember, just like that, I'm part of the fold. They pull me into every conversation and treat me as if I'm one of them.

Watch how she interacts with her kids and her family, somewhere along the way it clicks that she's at much more of a disadvantage than me with no hearing and she's able to do all of this. It's one thing for people to tell you something, saying it over and over until they're blue in the face. Yet until you experience it for yourself, then you get and the lesson is more meaningful.

His sister, Scarlett, sits down in the living room with me.

So why are you hiding? she asks.

I'm not quite sure what she means.

I'm not hiding.

You are. Corey told me that you're out here finding yourself while you left the woman you love worrying about you back home. You're hiding, but from what?

I'm not hiding. I just needed to prove to myself and to her that I could take care of myself. If I didn't have my voice, how I would be able to take care of her?

You really think she would be with you if she didn't think you could take care of yourself or take care of her? Does she seem to be like the kind of girl that wants to be taken care of?

She was my ASL teacher, that's how we met.

Helping people and taking care of them are two different things. You're running and you're hurting her while you do so. One thing I learned growing up, take no shit from anyone. If you walked back into my life after the way that you have been treating her, there would be no second chance. The longer you're here and the longer you're away from her, the less chance you have of getting her back. Unless, of course, self-sabotage was your plan from the start.

Then she gets up and rejoins her family in the kitchen while I sit there in shock. Pulling up my phone, I read Faith's messages and I see them in a new light. Has she just been texting me because she needed to know that I was okay, and have I missed my chance completely with her now? How badly did I screw things up, needing to find myself?

By the time Cory joins me in the living room. I've made the decision that it's time to go back. I don't want to be away from her any longer and don't want to chance losing her. Hopefully, I can make her understand. Otherwise, all this was for nothing.

Chapter 18

Faith

I read over that letter for what has to be the 100th time, looking for any clue that I might have missed.

Faith,

I've been thinking and when I see our future, I see us working as a team. I don't want you to have to take care of me. I want to be the one taking care of you. To be able to do that, I need to prove to myself that I can take care of myself, so that's what I'm setting out to do.

I don't know where I'm going or how long I'll be. I just need to know that I can do this on my own. But I will come back for you. When I come back, I will be a much better person and much better for you.

I have to do this not just for me but for us because I am head over heels in love with you and I won't be the person to drag you down.

I hope you'll wait for me.

Logan

After I got the letter, I tried texting and calling but he never picked up. I've sent a text every few days, hoping that maybe today will be the day I get a message or a reply, but I don't.

It's been hard for my brain to process. One minute we're planning our life together and our future and in the next, he's just gone. Out of my life, almost as if he never existed at all.

Noah said that they talked, and he understood why Logan had to do this. There's understanding and then there's talking about it. I would have supported him if he had just come to me and explained it. If he had said that we'd stay in contact and he wouldn't ignore me, I would have understood.

Not having any idea if he's safe, or if he's able to communicate with anyone, is upsetting enough. But with no way to reach him if I needed to is even worse. It's almost like he's a ghost.

Lexi decided that I needed a pick me up, so she scheduled one of her famous girls' nights. Noah and the guys are taking the baby and that leaves us girls to have fun and talk.

"All right, everyone's here, so let's move out to the sunroom and get the night started," Lexi says. Everyone follows the amazing smell of food that has been set out. There is both a Taco and Margarita bar.

"Make your food and sit down. Then I'm going to go over the rules, since we have some new faces here."

I'm pretty sure she means me and Lauren, as this is our first ladies' night. Well, officially anyway.

"Okay, ladies, here are the rules," Lexi says, holding up one finger. "One, no drinking and driving. There are guest bedrooms upstairs and downstairs and couches around the house so you can crash anywhere. You're welcome to pick any of those places."

She holds up a second finger. "Two, we are friends first. We are not bosses and employees. We are friends and we are here as friends. Venting about work is okay, venting about patients is okay, and venting about guys is encouraged. We are here to support each other." Then she holds up a third finger. "Three. What is talked about at ladies' night stays at ladies' night. This is a safe place. What is talked about in this room doesn't leave this room. Got it?"

We all nod, agreeing, and the other girls start talking. Brooke shares about what's going on with her sister-in-law and how she thinks they're finally starting to become friends with each other.

Paisley talks about the new girl her brother is dating and how everyone seems on edge after the last one. Lauren jumps in with talk of the wedding plans. When she's done, she looks over at me. I knew when she started talking that it was going to be my turn next. There's no way she was going to talk and let me slide by.

"I'm pretty sure Lauren is expecting me to talk about Logan. Unfortunately, I still haven't heard from him and have no idea if he's okay," I say, taking a sip of my margarita.

"Well, I can tell you he is fine because he checks in with Noah," Lexi cringes.

I feel my heart breaking.

"So, he just doesn't check in with me. I didn't want to believe that we were over, but I guess we are. Even though I thought he meant what he said in his letter, that he would be coming back, it doesn't look good. If he doesn't even check in with me letting me know that he's okay, but he's checking in with Noah, then I have no other choice than to believe that it was his way of breaking up with me," I say, fighting back the tears.

"That was not his intention at all." Lexi says, getting up and coming to my side.

"He's saying one thing, but his actions are saying something else. You don't ignore someone that you're in a relationship with so I'm glad he's okay, but I guess I'm not."

"These guys, when they leave the military and they come here, they have to reevaluate their whole lives. Not only do they have a lot to prove mostly to themselves, but they think they have to prove it to you too," Paisley says.

At her words, I shake my head because there's nothing they can say that will change my mind.

"Listen, I get that he could go out and prove whatever he needed to, but he could still check in, letting me know he's okay. Even better, he could have talked to me about it before up and leaving, allowing me to support him in his choice. But he did it and he's yet to check in with me, no matter how many texts I've sent. I know what ghosting is and should have recognized it sooner."

Tears that I've been trying to hold back fall. I don't even try to stop them. How could I have been such an idiot for so long? There I was thinking that he was coming back to me, when all along he was trying to let me down easy.

My brother was right. He bonded with me because he needed me and now that he doesn't need me, casts me aside. I was stupid enough to think that we had a future.

Now, I can't even face my brother and admit to him that he was right. That's the last thing I need because he'll start thinking he has the final say in any of my relationships. So I can't even call and talk to them. My mind's racing a million miles an hour when a glass is shoved into my hand.

"Here. Have something to drink. Since I haven't been drinking, I will drive and you can come stay with Gavin and me for a few days. That way, you're not alone, okay?" Lauren says.

Thinking what the hell, I throw back the Margarita, she just handed me.

Normally, I'm not a big drinker, so the tequila warms my body pretty fast. Somewhere in the back of my mind, I know I shouldn't have another one. So far, there's the one I just chugged, along with the one I had been sipping. Usually that's more than enough for me. I still grab another one. While the other girls talk and try to keep the conversations light, I just drink, feeling nothing. It's obvious everyone is slightly worried about me, but I don't care. Lexi keeps watching me like I'm a ticking time bomb and I think she's having a silent conversation with her husband, who I think is in the doorway behind me. But I don't care enough to turn around and find out.

True to her word, Lauren drives me to her home. I faintly remember Lexi saying something about leaving my car at her place. Right now, I could honestly care less as that's a problem for sober me, for the non-heartbroken me.

When we get to Lauren's house, Gavin is out on the front porch with his Seeing Eye dog. Even though he had surgery and gained some sight back, he's still legally blind. But he comes to help Lauren get me out of the car. Somewhere in the back of my head, I remember that their son is probably asleep in the house.

"Graham is spending the night at a friend's house," Lauren says.

"When the hell did you become a mind reader?" I snap back at her, causing Gavin to laugh.

"You just said that you need to be quiet because our son is inside," Lauren says.

"I didn't say that. I thought it."

"No you definitely said it out loud," Gavin chimes in.

"Well, of course you're going to take her side." I say.

"You really should get that front porch looked at. It's really wobbly," I tell them.

All they do is smile. What is with all the damn smiling tonight?

"Didn’t this used to be your son's playroom?"

"Yes, but he decided to move all his stuff to his room so that Grandma and Grandpa had a room when they came to visit." Lauren says, plopping me down on the bed.

"Well, isn't that sweet," I say drowsily.

After they say a few more things that are all muffled, I lie down and close my eyes.

From the moment my eyes close, all I see are the memories of Logan. When the tears start, I don't stop them this time.

Chapter 19

Logan

Despite my talk with Scarlett, I decided to stick around for a few more days. I wanted to look more into her life and how she manages just the basic daily communication. Plus, to be honest, I need a few days to figure out what to do and how I plan to handle the first time I see Faith after all these months.

Scarlett has been so generous, showing me how she gets along at work, with her kids, and her family. She has been very giving with her time and dealing with my sometimes stupid questions. At the end of every day, we end up at Corey's parents' house and all gather around an amazing home cooked meal. After dinner, Scarlett and I sit on the back porch and talk. Members of her family filter in and out, depending on what is going on.

How do you feel about your husband having to help you with things? I ask.

I have to trust my husband completely. A lot of the times it's easier for me to allow him to take the lead on things when we are out and about. It doesn't make me feel less than or incapable, it actually makes me feel loved and taken care of. Though it did take me a while to get to that point.

I am always worried that Faith will see me as someone that she needs to take care of. Eventually, she will get sick of being a caregiver and move on.

But isn't that our job in relationships to care for our significant other? My husband and I took marriage vows. It means that we've pledged our lives to each other, to help each other when the other one needs it. To be the other one's support and to allow them to help us when we need it. So, it goes both ways. If she got sick and God forbid diagnosed with cancer, would you walk away from her because she needed treatment?

God no! That's when Faith would need me the most. I am disgusted with the idea that I would abandon her.

Exactly, so why would she walk away in the moments when you need her? If you love her, you must have the trust that she is there for you in the good times and the bad. In return, she offers you the same trust that you will be there for her anytime that she needs you.

Each night we would have a conversation and she would give me a lot to think about. She has a way of asking questions that makes me think of things in a new light. Without ever making me believe that I'm wrong, she challenges my way of thinking.

When I got to Cory's parents' house today, I knew that I wanted to talk to her husband. I had to get the perspective from his point of view.

After dinner, we headed to the back porch to sit down and talk.

You are going to ask me what it's like to be on the other end of things. To be the one that she relies on and to be the translator as she needs it, aren't you? He says, being straight forward.

Of course, I want to know the other side of the coin. Maybe it's different because I'm a man and feel like I should be taking care of her and not the other way around.

Scarlett has had those same thoughts. Should she be taking care of me since I'm the main breadwinner, even though she works?

Maybe it's just human nature that we don't like depending on other people, I say.

Honestly, I think you have to realize that you are taking care of her the same way Scarlett takes care of me. I may have to assist her from time to time, but she's there to help take care of the kids. Hell, she was the one that gave me kids. I couldn't have carried them. Also, she's the one that does the grocery shopping, cooks dinner, and keeps my schedule organized. I don't know how many appointments I would miss or things I would miss if she didn't. He shakes his head with a smile on his face.

She takes care of me in more ways than she realizes, and I wish that I could make her see that. So if translating and helping her more in our marriage is what I can do to repay it, then I'm more than happy to. To be completely honest, one of the hardest things is to step back and watch her struggle, knowing that I have to wait for her to ask for help. You have to keep communication open and keep talking.

I think about just how different our situations are. Things really are reversed when I'm the one that needs help versus his wife.

You really should have this conversation with her because I guarantee you there's ways that you help her that you don't even realize. His words stop me from going too far down that road.

That's the thing. I don't help her. I feel like more of a hindrance. She's the one that had to teach me how to communicate with the outside world again. She taught me sign language and pushed me to make friends. I don't know what I've done for her, and that scares me.

You have loved her. Don't you realize that's all she needs is to be loved unconditionally? If you can't say that you love her unreservedly and completely, then you need to let her go and find someone who will.

His words are a hard slap in the face. I have loved her unconditionally and with my whole heart. The thought of someone else doing that makes me sick to my stomach and ready to punch someone.

After going back to my temporary hotel room, I need to think about everything. Then it's as if fate has decided to step in. Because I get a text from Noah that shakes me.

Noah: The girls are having ladies' night here and Faith knows that you have been in contact with me and not her.

Me: How did she find out?

Noah: The girls have been drinking and Lexi let it slip. You should know that she thinks that you don't care about her because she hasn't gotten even one single text.

Me: It's not that simple, though.

Noah: I know, but those are her words and I kind of agree. Not even sending one to let her know you are okay is kind of a dick move. Lauren took her home, but she's crying her eyes out and is convinced that you broke up with her. She thinks you ghosted her, by letting her down easily.

Me: Fuck.

Noah: Yeah, I'd offer to help, but this is a hole you dug yourself into and it's one that you are going to need to take yourself out of.

I never had any intention of leaving her or ending things with her. The fact that she would think that after everything that we had together, breaks my heart.

Maybe I should have waited and talked to her face to face. Would it have given her comfort knowing I was coming back to her? Though I really thought doing it this way was for the best.

Spending the last few days with Scarlett and her husband has given me a newfound confidence that I desperately needed.

But now I'm ready to fight.

I hope Faith gets a good night's sleep tonight because she's going to need it.

Chapter 20

Faith

I'm working with a new guy at Oakside, and took him out to the garden because he's getting frustrated. Though, I expected it to happen because it's not easy when your world is turned upside down.

All the men and women who have been injured and end up at Oakside have a tragic story. Some of them are as simple as they were involved in an explosion or in Logan's case, a plane crash which caused injuries from which they now have to heal.

Those injuries are a little easier to heal from because it's people like them and they can bond and grow and become friends.

But then you get the guys like Easton and this new guy that I'm working with, Mike, who were prisoners of war.

If you try to dig too far into them, their stories will break your heart. Mike and I have been working together for the last week. He wasn't a prisoner of war as long as Easton. Nevertheless, he currently has his jaw wired shut because it had been dislocated. He's had multiple surgeries, and sadly, there are a few more in his future.

The chances are really high that he'll be able to speak again, but until then, he needs to know some basic skills to communicate. That is where I come in.

Bringing him out here to the garden will be a nice change of scenery for him, and the fresh air can't hurt. He seems to be enjoying it. I'm glad for him but for myself, I'm starting to regret it. All I can see out here is Logan. This was our spot where we would come and have many of our lessons. This is where I fell in love with him.

It wasn't just talking to him but watching the way he'd enjoy the little things, like being in the sun or watching butterflies in the garden. When I asked him about it, he said having been so close to death with the plane crash made him realize how lucky he was to be alive.

But right now, I need to focus on Mike, and can't think about Logan. I'm concentrating so hard on Mike, I ignore the footsteps that are coming up behind us. Assuming it's just another patient, I check over my shoulder to make sure we're not in his or her way and I'm absolutely shocked to find Logan standing there watching us.

"What are you doing here?" I ask him. Then I turn to Mike to fill him in.

"I'm sorry. This is my ex-boyfriend. I never expected him to show up like this, and haven't heard from him in weeks."

Sweetheart, I am far from your ex-boyfriend. Don't ever use that term for me again, Logan says, not looking the least bit happy about it.

You ghosted me. You went and left and didn't even let me know if you were okay. Yet you were in contact with everyone else but me. That pretty much constitutes a breakup. I sign because I don't want to draw attention to the fight we are having.

Well, I'm here to prove differently. Who is this? He nods towards Mike.

"This is Mike. Mike, this is Logan. I've been working with him for the last week," I say. I'm not using ASL because I don't want to be rude to Mike since he's still learning and would have no idea what we're saying in sign language.

Will you translate for me? Logan asks.

"He just asked for me to translate for him," I tell Mike.

I was a Navy pilot and a patient here at Oakside. After the plane crash, I lost my voice, he says, pulling down the collar of his shirt to show the scar on his neck.

One thing I know is how isolated you feel right now. Not being able to communicate is lonely and I felt the same way. There were days that it felt hopeless, like I was never going to catch on to what everyone was trying to teach me. Some days I would watch the videos that Faith suggested, and my eyes would glaze over, trying to understand what they were saying. More often than not, I wanted to give up.

As I'm translating for Logan, my heart is breaking because I never knew all this. Why didn't he write this in the journal that I got to read?

The best parts of my day were when I got to see Faith and being here in the garden. I wanted to impress her, so I studied hard. Then one day out of nowhere, it all clicked. So don't give up and just keep studying because it will pay off. In the meantime, don't push away people that are here and trying to help you.

I wait to see Mike's reaction, and it takes a moment, but he just nods. Though I wonder if any of that got through to him, and if it did, will it make a difference?

When you're done here, can we talk? I'll wait on the front porch for you, Logan says, watching me and waiting for an answer.

Nodding, I turn back to give Mike my full attention. Mike doesn't bring up Logan again and for that, I am thankful. In an attempt to avoid Logan for a little longer, I spend longer with Mike than I normally would. If Mike noticed, he didn't bring it up, and I need to remember to thank him for that at some point.

When I leave Mike's room, I take my time and go down to what used to be the basement and is now Lexi and Noah's office space. It also has the kitchen and some employee rooms.

"Did you see Logan is here?" Noah says as I step into Lexi's office.

I don't know why they have separate offices, as they are normally together in one.

"Why don't you two just make this your joint office and do something else with Noah's office? Do you really ever work there?" I joke with them.

"We talked about it. Now stop ignoring the question." Lexi looks up from the computer, staring me down.

"Yes, he found me and is waiting on the front porch for me. Though I'm not sure I even want to see him, not that I have a choice. I definitely have no idea what to say to him." I sigh, sitting down in the chair in front of Lexi's desk.

"You don't really have to say anything. Just listen to what he has to say. Let him speak his piece and get whatever he has to say off his chest. You don't even have to react to what he says. Today you can say you need time to think it over," Lexi says. She's obviously trying to be the supportive.

"But he did come all this way to talk to you. Though I may not agree with the way he went about things, I understand why he did it," Noah says, giving me the male point of view. Lexi smacks his arm lightly and playfully, but enough to get his attention.

"The last thing she needs to say is that she understands why he did it. The reason why doesn't matter, it's the fact that he did and how she is going to be able to move forward. Regardless of his intentions, her feelings now are what matters." Lexi says.

"Angel, we're not going to fight about someone else's problems. We can be Switzerland, support them both and let them figure it out," Noah says.

It makes me smile at how sweet they are. I'd give anything for a love like theirs and for a while I thought I had it with Logan, but now I'm not so sure.

"Stop stalling. Get out there. We are getting ready to go home. You're more than welcome to stop by if you need to talk afterward," Lexi says.

Reluctantly, I say goodbye and go to the front porch secretly hoping that maybe he decided to leave and talk on another day. But just like he promised, he's sitting in one of the rocking chairs on the front porch watching people in the front yard.

When he sees me walking towards him, he gives me a brilliant smile that lights up his face. Standing, he hesitantly reaches to hug me, and I let him, but I don't hug back.

You have no idea how much I've missed you. I don't know if it's possible, but somehow you have gotten more beautiful, and I really appreciate you listening to what I have to say.

"Well, let's get on with it so I can get home," I say, sitting in the chair next to him.

Chapter 21

Logan

When she joins me on the porch, it's easy to see she has her walls up and she has every right to. If she truly thinks that the way I left, I was trying to ghost her, then she should protect herself. But I am here to prove otherwise.

It's obvious she was uncomfortable with the hug, but I didn't think I just knew I needed her in my arms.

"What do you want, Logan?" She crosses her arms over her chest as she sits down in the rocking chair next to mine. But she perches on the edge, signaling she's ready to stand and walk away from me quickly. But she won't get away and we won't ever be done, I won't let us. I will always fight for her, for us.

I have always wanted a family, a wife to come home to, kids to snuggle up and watch TV with. But in my head, it was always me being the one to take care of everyone. That hasn't changed. I see you in my life now and I had to know that not only could I take care of you, but I could take care of myself. I had to prove it to myself.

"If you had just told me, I would have supported you. And if you could have at least checked in every now and then to let me know that you were okay. Or hell, responded to one of my, sadly, many texts. That would have been great. But disappearing the way you did, that wasn't okay. How you made me feel like I was worthless to you is not all right."

My heart sinks at hearing those words because that was never my intention and I, for sure, never thought it would make her feel that way in a million years.

With every instinct in my body, I want to wrap her in my arms, hold her tight and swear on everything worth a damn that was never my intent.

I never meant to make you feel that way. Because to me, you are the most important and precious thing in the world. I just knew if you begged me not to go that I wouldn't go. And I had to do this for us. But more importantly, I had to do this for me.

"Do what?" she asks. But her face softens a fraction. If I had blinked, I'd have missed it.

Just normal everyday things. I ordered food from a restaurant and went to the movies, got a job and got a place to stay...

"Wait, wait, you got a job and you moved someplace else? You moved away from me?"

There's a look on her face that I can't quite read, but there's definitely hurt mixed in with whatever else she is feeling. I can see where her mind is going this time. She thinks I moved away from her and that just isn't true.

For weeks, I lived in a crap motel because it was only temporary.

It was just temporary, and I no longer work there because I am here and I'm not going anywhere.

"How do I trust that you're not going to just pack up and leave again to find yourself, or because I'm not enough?"

Faith, you have to understand that you gave me so much, teaching me how to communicate with the world again. But I had to put that to use. To know that I could do it and I could do it without help from anyone. Now I've proven it to myself, so there is no reason for me to leave. What's more, I don't want to be apart from you again. Not one single day for the rest of our lives.

If I thought for even a moment I could get her to agree to marry me now, I'd drop to both knees and beg. I'd rip my heart out and lay it at her feet. Whatever she needs to get through this, I will do. Because we will get through this, there is no other option.

I know my Faith though, and when she goes home tonight, she will start thinking it all over. She will see it from my point of view, maybe have some questions, but I will be right there to answer them for her.

"I'm hurt, Logan, with what you did. Still even with you standing right here in front of me, I need to find a way to believe that you're not going to just up and walk out on me again. How do I find that type of trust?"

It's not for you to find, it's for me to prove and I will if you give me the chance.

She stands up, takes a few steps away, and I think she's going to get up and leave me there. Even though she would have every right to do just that, I'm not going to let her go so easily. I will chase her and show her that I am here and I'm not going anywhere. Through my actions, I am prepared to show her my love and appreciation for her every day for the rest of my life.

Stopping at the edge of the porch, she looks out over the lawn with her back towards me. The sun is on her face and I'm sure it feels amazing with the weather that we've been having.

I feel numb without her. Now I realize I have felt numb for weeks. Right now, the only way to fix it was to get my girl back. To be back in her arms and I knew this moment wouldn't be easy, but I didn't expect it to be this hard, either.

Neither one of us says a word and I sit there without making a sound, hoping that she's thinking about what I said and it will lead her back to me.

"What is this about going out and proving you still have it? And to know that women will still want you before you settled down with me?" she asks, turning back around.

Fuck no! There was no one else! That was the furthest thing from my mind. Because in my mind, you are the one settling with me. I know how fucking lucky I am to have you in my life. I. Love. You.

I try to make my point clear, and I hope I have when her eyes start to water. Now I have to go for broke, knowing I did everything I possibly could.

I want to marry you. I want to build a life with you and want to have kids with you. I want to grow old, with you. There isn't one thing in the world I want to do without you by my side. This life isn't worth living if you aren't with me.

She turns, putting her back toward me and stares out at the front yard. It feels like hours stretch between us when, in reality, it's only a minute, maybe two, before she turns back around.

"I can give you time, but it's not going to be like it was before."

I'll take whatever you can give me, and I promise that I'm here to stay.

She nods and sits back down where she was before.

"If you're planning on staying, what are your plans?"

Knowing she'd want proof that I had plans to stay, so I made sure that I had all my ducks in a row before I even came to see her. In short, there is no way in hell I was coming without a plan. Though once again that means that Noah and Lexi knew before she did, but they swore to keep it quiet.

Lexi and Noah have an apartment in their basement that they're going to let me stay in. I'll be starting school in Savannah soon and the money that the VA will give me for that will allow me to concentrate solely on school.

I was hesitant to sign a lease for a year because I'm hoping that by the time I'll be ready to move into something more permanent. Because then, it will be because Faith and I are moving in together.

When I told Noah, he jumped at the chance to offer me the apartment at their place. Lexi is pretty certain that it's not going to take Faith an entire year to come around to the idea of us getting married.

I get it. I wasn't expecting things to go back to the way that they were before. When I left, things were messed up in my head and I wasn't in the best space. Without a doubt, I wasn't thinking like I should. But that's no excuse for what I did to you. For what I did to us.

"Logan, for the record, I love you, too."

When she says those words, I feel like I'm flying. I dreamed about her saying those words to me, but to hear them out loud makes me feel like I'm actually worthy of them.

I know she said things aren't going back to the way they were and I completely agree. But this woman who I love more than anything in the world, this woman who I want to spend the rest of my life with, just said she loves me. There's no way I can sit here and act like it's not a huge deal because to me, it's everything.

Standing, I pull her into my arms and the moment she looks up at me, I kiss her passionately. Even though I don't know if she's going to allow me to kiss her, or if she's going to push me away. I don't care. Because I need her to know what hearing those words do to me.

While I don't know if she's more shocked that I kissed her or if I'm more shocked that she didn't push me away. But when I finally pull back from that kiss, she's breathing just as hard as I am. Our bodies definitely remember each other even if our hearts are a little bruised.

Let me take you out to dinner on a real date. I want to pick you up at your house, wine and dine you like our first date should have been.

"You have a car?" she asks, her voice soft.

Yes, it was the first thing I purchased. So, can I take you out, sweetheart?

"Yes, I would like that. I'm free tomorrow night."

I will be there. Wear something nice. We're going to do this right.

Nodding, she walks away with a smile and a blush on her face. If I had asked her out the right way from the beginning, I wonder if she would have had that same look. It's not a look of someone who's settling and for the first time I start to believe that she really wants me for me.

Chapter 22

Faith

It's been a few weeks since Logan came back, and I've been able to watch him flourish. He is so much more confident now. I always knew at some point he would gain his confidence and I couldn't wait to see it. This man is twenty times sexier with his boldness and conviction in us. He believes strongly that there is no other option than for us to work out, to have a future together.

Every day, no matter what his schedule is, he makes sure that he sees me. Some days it's him visiting me at Oakside while I work. Mike likes those days because the two of them get on really well and they're able to have a conversation together.

Other days, he picks me up and takes me out on a date. I've met him in Savannah to have lunch in between some of his classes, and other times he's at my place and we're snuggling watching TV on the couch.

Every morning when I get up, there is a text that says hello beautiful. I hope you have an amazing day. I love you. Every night before bed, he tells me to have sweet dreams and how much he loves me and thanking me for whatever it is we got to do that day.

I've laid in bed at night and wondered if all this was just a show and as soon as I cave, then he would stop. Because it's the thrill of the chase, right?

But that just is not my Logan. I've talked to Lexi about it too, and she agrees. She reminded me that I never really got to know Logan outside the walls of Oakside, so I never got to see him in full on relationship mode. That's true and she's right, I hadn't seen this side of Logan. It's all new to me.

Not only is Logan making an effort with me, he's been spending time with my family, too. Both with me there and without me. He understood how my brother was hesitant about him, so he spent time with my brother letting him get to know him. Along the way, he's completely won my brother over.

Lexi is completely on Logan's side as well and makes no effort in hiding it when she talks to me the nights that I'm not with him. Since he's been living with Lexi and Noah, she's gotten to know him and they both have taken a liking to him.

Many sleepless nights, I've sat and thought about why Logan did what he did and why he needed to prove it to himself. After talking to Lauren about it and hell, I've even talked to a few of my past clients, I'm more understanding. All of them basically say that overcoming that milestone of using what they learned after the military in the real world was the biggest hurdle that they faced.

They all handled it differently. Some just wanted to get back into their normal routine as quickly as possible. While others did like Logan, and went cold turkey into an environment they had no idea about proving they could flourish anywhere. How I didn't know this, I'll never know. Lauren says it's because by the time they hit that point, I had moved on to my next client. It's not often we get to see the completed behind-the-scenes picture as care providers.

Tonight, Logan and I have been asked to have dinner with Lexi and Noah. By the time that I arrive, Logan is waiting on the front porch for me. He looks so comfortable and relaxed on the front porch swing in the shade of the big oak trees in the front yard.

Standing, he greets me as I pull into the driveway. When I step out of my car, as always, he has a huge smile on his face, one that lights up his eyes. After giving me a hug and a short soft kiss on the lips, he wraps an arm around my waist and leads me up the steps, but stops me before we hit the front door.

I think things between us are going pretty good, don't you? he asks.

"Yes, I think they're going very good."

Somehow, that makes his smile even brighter.

Good. I want to ask you something.

"Anything." I see the moment his nerves hit him, and my mind starts to race with what he could possibly have to ask me that would make him this nervous.

But the instant he drops to one knee, I know.

I knew from our first kiss that you were the woman I wanted to marry. I never wavered in that belief, and I've never been so sure of anything in my life. You are one of the kindest, caring and generous people I have ever met. You believed in me even when I didn't. You've made me the happiest person in the world, and I want to spend the rest of my life making you just as happy.

Then he pulls a ring out of his pocket and holds it up for me to see. It is by far the most gorgeous ring I've ever seen in my life, and larger than anything I've ever worn. It has a vintage feel to it and the way that it glitters off the light it's breathtaking.

Will you marry me?

Taking a minute, I want to memorize this moment in time. The look he's giving me, the way I feel, how my heart's racing, and finally, the way the light hits his hair. I want to remember every single detail.

"Yes!"

He jumps up and slides the ring onto my finger.

I can't wait to see you walking down the aisle to me in a beautiful white dress. Ever since our first kiss, I've been dreaming of that moment.

This time when he kisses me so intensely and passionately, the sparks are so fierce that I can hardly stand. Already I know that my relationship with this man is going to get better and better over time. How the kiss at our wedding will top this one, is something I can wait to experience.

Epilogue

Zane

Watching people's mouths move but not being able to hear a word of it is a very odd sensation. Sometimes they just try to speak louder and over pronounce their words, thinking that maybe I'll be able to read their lips but I can't.

Up until a few weeks ago, I had my hearing. Then one bombing later, not only do I have some scars, but my world has gone completely silent.

I've gotten some sick entertainment by watching people give up trying to get me to understand them and finally write what they have to say. This nurse is smart, though. She pulls out her phone and uses the text to speech before turning it around and letting me read it.

They will be here later today to transport you to Oakside. They've got someone there that will teach you sign language. Your doctor visits and physical therapy will all be on site. Do you have any questions?

Shaking my head no seems to satisfy her. I guess handing me a pamphlet on Oakside is easier than trying to explain it to someone who can't hear you.

The place looks interesting. Kind of like a fancy bed-and-breakfast for healing injured military personnel. I have to say the food promised to be a hell of a lot better than the barely identifiable meat substance I was given for lunch today.

I look over the pamphlet again as I wait for them to come in and get me. When the nurse finally shows up, she insists on pushing me down in a wheelchair with all my stuff in my lap. A long time ago, I learned not to fight them on things like this. Man, just climb into the wheelchair and let them take me wherever we're going.

The ride over to Oakside is fairly easy, and it's nice to see something other than the walls of a hospital.

At least once I get to Oakside, they're not insisting on a wheelchair anymore. A man with a bunch of scars walks up with a beautiful blonde by his side. Then he hands me a piece of paper.

I'm Noah and this is my wife, Lexi. We run Oakside and we'll be showing you to your room. Let us know if you need anything at any point. We've supplied your room with a whiteboard, washable markers, plenty of pads, paper, pens, and journals.

Nodding, I smile. I haven't tried to talk since losing my hearing. I figure there's no point in it. They show me to my room, and they aren't gone more than a minute before another couple knocks on the door.

This one's holding a tablet and hands it to me to read.

I'm Faith and this is Logan, my fiancé. Logan was a patient here and had lost his voice. I taught him ASL and different tricks to communicate with the outside world, and that's what I am here to teach you as well. This tablet is yours. I figure it's probably easier to communicate than writing on a whiteboard and paper all the time. At least Logan thought so. I will give you a few days to settle in and we will start on Monday.

Once again, I gave her a nod and a small smile. This seems to appease her and they both leave the room.

At least the people here at Oakside seem pretty chipper and they seem to be go getters. Hopefully, that translates into my healing process as well.

Not that anything's really going to help. It's not like I'll be able to hear again or have my life back. Not that I have much to live for, anyway. The Navy Seals were my whole life, and before this blast they were trying to convince me to retire at the ripe old age of thirty-nine.

Even at thirty-nine, I had no idea what I wanted to do with the rest of my life. I always thought that the Navy Seals were my game plan. I didn't have anyone in my life, just some family that I talked to occasionally. Now that I can't hear jack shit, I really have absolutely no idea what I plan to do with my life. But like my dad likes to constantly remind me, I better figure it the fuck out pretty fast.

Deciding to go for a walk, I explore the place. Lexi catches me and starts scribbling something down on a piece of paper.

The gardens outside are really beautiful. If you want to go for a walk, they're outside the front door and to the left.

I follow her directions but never make it that far. Instead, I stop in my tracks when I see the woman lying in the grass staring at Oakside with a sketch pad in her lap.

She's way too young for me, but something says even though I don't know what my future holds, somehow she's part of it.

• • • • • ● • ● • • • •

Want more Logan and Faith? **Grab a bonus Epilogue when you join my newsletter!**

Get the next Oakside Book, **Saving Zane!**

Start reading Oakside from the beginning with **Saving Noah**

Other Books by Kaci Rose

See all of Kaci Rose's Books

Oakside Military Heroes Series

Saving Noah – Lexi and Noah

Saving Easton – Easton and Paisley

Saving Teddy – Teddy and Mia

Saving Levi – Levi and Mandy

Saving Gavin – Gavin and Lauren

Saving Logan – Logan and Faith

Oakside Shorts

Saving Mason - Mason and Paige

Saving Ethan – Bri and Ethan

Mountain Men of Whiskey River

Take Me To The River – Axel and Emelie

Take Me To The Cabin – Pheonix and Jenna
Take Me To The Lake – Cash and Hope
Taken by The Mountain Man - Cole and Jana
Take Me To The Mountain – Bennett and Willow
Take Me To The Edge – Storm

Mountain Men of Mustang Mountain
(Series Written with Dylann Crush and Eve London)
February is for Ford – Ford and Luna
April is for Asher – Asher and Jenna

Club Red – Short Stories
Daddy's Dare – Knox and Summer
Sold to my Ex's Dad - Evan and Jana
Jingling His Bells – Zion and Emma

Club Red: Chicago
Elusive Dom

Chasing the Sun Duet
Sunrise – Kade and Lin
Sunset – Jasper and Brynn

Rock Stars of Nashville
She's Still The One – Dallas and Austin

Standalone Books

Texting Titan - Denver and Avery
Accidental Sugar Daddy – Owen and Ellie
Stay With Me Now – David and Ivy
Midnight Rose - Ruby and Orlando
Committed Cowboy – Whiskey Run Cowboys
Stalking His Obsession - Dakota and Grant
Falling in Love on Route 66 - Weston and Rory
Billionaire's Marigold - Mari and Dalton

Connect with Kaci Rose

Website

Facebook

Kaci Rose Reader's Facebook Group

TikTok

Instagram

Twitter

Goodreads

Book Bub

Join Kaci Rose's VIP List (Newsletter)

About Kaci Rose

Kaci Rose writes steamy contemporary romances mostly set in small towns. She grew up in Florida but now lives in a cabin in the mountains of East Tennessee. She is a mom to 5 kids, a rescue dog who is scared of his own shadow, an energetic young German Shepard who is still in training, and 2 barn cats who she has to stop her kids from trying to pet constantly.

She also writes steamy cowboy romances as Kaci M. Rose.

Please Leave a Review!

I love to hear from my readers! Please **head over to your favorite store and leave a review** of what you thought of this book!

Made in the USA
Columbia, SC
23 September 2024